The Honorable
Miss Moonlight

The Honorable Miss Moonlight

Onoto Watanna

MINT EDITIONS

The Honorable Miss Moonlight was first published in 1912.

This edition published by Mint Editions 2021.

ISBN 9781513208992 | E-ISBN 9781513276557

Published by Mint Editions®

MINT
EDITIONS

minteditionbooks.com

Publishing Director: Jennifer Newens
Design & Production: Rachel Lopez Metzger
Project Manager: Micaela Clark
Typesetting: Westchester Publishing Services

Contents

I

The day had been long and sultry. It was the season of little heat, when an all-encompassing humidity seemed suspended over the land. Sky and earth were of one monotonous color, a dim blue, which faded to shadowy grayness at the fall of the twilight.

With the approach of evening, a soothing breeze crept up from the river. Its faint movement brought a measure of relief, and nature took on a more animated aspect.

Up through the narrow, twisting roads, in and out of the never-ending paths, the lights of countless jinrikishas twinkled, bound for the Houses of Pleasure. Revelers called to each other out of the balmy darkness. Under the quivering light of a lifted lantern, suspended for an instant, faces gleamed out, then disappeared back into the darkness.

To the young Lord Saito Gonji the night seemed to speak with myriad tongues. Like some finely tuned instrument whose slenderest string must vibrate if touched by a breath, so the heart of the youth was stirred by every appeal of the night. He heard nothing of the chatter and laughter of those about him. For the time at least, he had put behind him that sickening, deadening thought that had borne him company now for so long. He was giving himself up entirely to the brief hour of joy, which had been agreeably extended to him in extenuation of the long life of thralldom yet to come.

It was in his sole honor that the many relatives and connections of his family had assembled, joyously to celebrate the fleeting hours of youth. For within a week the Lord Saito Gonji was to marry. Upon this pale and dreamy youth the hopes of the illustrious house of Saito depended. To him the august ancestors looked for the propagating of their honorable seed. He was the last of a great family, and had been cherished and nurtured for one purpose only.

With almost as rigid care as would have been bestowed upon a novitiate priest, Gonji had been educated.

"Send the child you love upon a journey," admonished the stern-hearted Lady Saito Ichigo to her husband; and so at the early age of five the little Gonji was sent to Kummumotta, there to be trained under the strictest discipline known to the samourai. Here he developed in strength and grace of body; but, seemingly caught in some intangible web, the mind of the youth awoke not from its dreams. His arm had the strength of the samourai, said his teachers, but his spirit and his heart were those of the poet.

There came a period when he was placed in the Imperial University, and a new life opened to the wondering youth. New laws, new modes of thought, the alluring secrets of strange sciences, baffling and fascinating, all opened their doors to the infatuated and eager Gonji. With the enthusiasm born of his solitary years, the boy grasped avidly after the ideals of the New Japan. His career in college was notable. In him professor and student recognized the born leader and genius. He was to do great things for Japan some day!

Then came a time when the education of the youth was abruptly halted, and he was ordered to return to his home. While his mind was still engaged in the fascinating employment of planning a career, his parents ceremoniously presented him to Ohano, a girl he had known from childhood and a distant relative of his mother's family. Mechanically and obediently the dazed Gonji found himself exchanging with the maiden the first gifts of betrothal.

Ohano was plump, with a round, somewhat sullen face, a pouting, full-lipped mouth, and eyes so small they seemed but mere slits in her face. She had inherited the inscrutable, disdainful expression of her lofty ancestors.

Though he had played with her as a child and had seen her upon every occasion during his school vacations, Gonji looked at her now with new eyes. As a little boy he had liked Ohano. She was his sole playmate, and it had been his delight to tease her. Now, as he watched her stealthily, he was consumed with a sense of unutterable despair. Could it be that his fairest dreams were to end with Ohano?

Like every other Japanese youth, who knows that some day his proper mate will be chosen and given to him, Gonji had conjured up a lovely, yielding creature of the imagination, a gentle, smiling, mysterious Eve, who, like a new world, should daily surprise and delight him. As he looked at Ohano, sitting placidly and contentedly by his side, he was conscious only of an inner tumult of rebellion and repulsion against the chains they were forging inexorably about him and this girl. It was impossible, he felt, to drag him nearer to her. The very thought revolted, stunned him, and suddenly, rudely, he turned his back upon his bride.

The relatives agreed that something should be done to offset the gloom of the first stages of betrothal. It was suggested that the bridegroom have a full week of freedom. As was the custom among many, he should for the first time be introduced to the life of gaiety and pleasure that lay outside the lofty, ancestral walls, the better, later, to appreciate the calm and pure joys of home and family.

In single file the jinrikishas had been running along a narrow road which overlooked city and bay. Now they swerved into shadowy by-paths and plunged into the heart of the woods. A velvety darkness, through which the drivers picked their way with caution, enwrapped them.

For some time the tingling music of samisen and drum close by had been growing ever clearer. Suddenly the glimmer of many lights was seen, as if suspended overhead. Almost unconsciously faces were raised, excited breaths drawn in admiration and approval. Like a great sparkling jewel hung in mid-air, the House of Slender Pines leaned over its wooded terraces toward them.

Gay little mousmés, rubbing hands and knees together, ran to meet them at the gate, kowtowing and hissing in obeisance. The note of a samisen was heard; and a thin little voice, sweet, and incredibly high, broke into song. Geishas, with great flowers in their hair, fell into a posturing group, dancing with hand, head, and fan. Gonji watched them in a fascinated silence, noting the minutest detail of their attire, their expression, their speech. They belonged to a world which, till now, he had not been permitted even to explore. Nay, till but recently he had been rigidly guarded from even the slightest possible contact with these little creatures of joy. Soon he was to be set in the niche destined for him by his ancestors. Here was his sole opportunity to seize the fleeting delights of youth.

A laughing-faced mousmé, red-lipped and with saucy, teasing eyes that peeped at him from beneath veiled lashes, knelt to hold his sake-tray. He leaned gravely toward the girl and examined her face with a curious wonder; but her smile brought no response to the somewhat sad and somber lips of the young man, nor did he even deign to sip the fragrant cup she tendered.

An elder cousin offered some chaffing advice, and an hilarious uncle suggested that the master of the house put his geishas upon parade; but the father of Gonji roughly interposed, declaring that his son's thoughts, naturally, were elsewhere. It was so with all expectant bridegrooms. His father's words awoke the boy from his dreaming. He turned very pale and trembled. His head drooped forward, and he felt an irresistible inclination to cover his face with his hands. His father's voice sounded in gruff whisper at his ear:

"Pay attention. You see now the star of the night. It is the famous Spider, spinning her web!"

As Gonji slowly raised his head and gazed like one spellbound at the dancer, his father added, with a sudden vehemence:

"Take care, my son, lest she entrap thee, too, like the proverbial fly."

A hush had fallen upon the gardens. Almost it seemed as if the tiny feet of the dancer stirred not at all. Yet, with imperceptible advances, she moved nearer and nearer to her fascinated audience. Above her flimsy gown of sheerest veiling, which sprang like a web on all sides and above her, her face shone with its marvelous beauty and allurement. Her lips were apart, smiling, coaxing, teasing; and her eyes, wide and very large, seemed to seek over the heads of her audience for the one who should prove her prey. It was the final motion of the dance of the Spider, the seeking for, the finding, the seizing of her imaginary victim. Now the Spider's eyes had ceased to wander. They were fixed compellingly upon those of the Lord Saito Gonji.

He had arisen to his feet, and with a half-audible exclamation—a sound of an indrawn sigh—he advanced toward the dancer. For a moment, breathlessly, he stood close beside her. The subtle odor of her perfumed hair and body stole like a charm over his senses. Her sleeve fluttered against his hand for but the fraction of a moment, yet thrilled and tormented him. He looked at the Spider with the eyes of one who sees a new and radiant wonder. Then darkness came rudely between them. The geisha's face vanished with the light. He was standing alone, staring into the darkness, his father's voice droning meaninglessly in his ear.

II

Her real name was as poetical as the one she was known by was forbidding and repelling. Moonlight, it was; though all the gay world which hovers about a famous geisha, like flies over the honey-pot, knew her solely as the "Spider."

"Spider" she was called because of the peculiar dance she had originated. It was against all classical precedents, but of so exceptional a character that in a night, a single hour, as it were, she found herself from a humble little apprentice the most celebrated geisha in Kioto, that paradise of geishas.

It was a day of golden fortune for Matsuda, who owned the girl. She had been bound to his service since the age of seven with bonds as drastic as if the days of slavery still existed.

Harsh, cunning, even cruel to the many girls in his employ, Matsuda had yet one vulnerable point. That was his overwhelming affection for the geisha he had married, and she was afflicted with a malady of the brain. Some said it was due to the death of her many children, all of whom had succumbed to an infectious disease. From whatever misfortune, the gentle Okusama, as they called her in the geisha-house, was at intervals blank-minded. Still she, the harmless, gentle creature, was loved by the geishas; and, as far as it lay in her power, she was their friend, and often saved them from the wrath of Matsuda. It was into her empty bosom the little Moonlight had crept and found a warm and loving home. With a yearning as deep as though the child were her own, the wife of Matsuda watched over the child. It was under her tutelage that Moonlight learned all the arts of an accomplished geisha. In her time the wife of Matsuda had been very famous, too, and no one knew better than she, soft of mind and witless as she was at times, the dances and the songs of the geisha-house.

Matsuda had watched with some degree of irritation, not unmixed with a peculiar jealousy, his wife's absorption in the tiny Moonlight. He did not approve of gentle treatment toward a mere apprentice. It was only by harsh measures that a girl could properly learn the severe profession. Later, when she had mastered all the intricate arts and graces, then, perhaps, one might prove lenient. It was no uncommon thing for a geisha to be pampered and spoiled, but an apprentice, never!

However, the child seemed to make happier the lot of the beloved Okusama, and there was nothing to be done about the matter.

Disliking the child, Matsuda nevertheless recognized from the first her undoubted beauty, the thing which had induced him, in fact, to pay an exceptional price to her guardians for her. He had little faith in her future as a geisha, however, since his wife chose to pet and protect her. How was it possible for her to learn from the poor, witless Okusama? When the latter joyously jabbered of the little one's wonderful progress, Matsuda would smile or grunt surlily.

Then, one day, walking in the woods, he had come, unexpectedly, upon the posturing child, tossing her little body from side to side like a wind-blown flower, while his wife picked two single notes upon the samisen. Matsuda watched them dumb-smitten. Was it possible, he asked himself, that the Okusama had discovered what he had overlooked? But he brushed the thought aside. These were merely the precocious antics of a spoiled child. They would not be pretty in one grown to womanhood. There was much to do in the geisha-house. The fame of his gardens must be kept assiduously before the public. Matsuda had no time for the little Moonlight, save, chidingly, to frown upon her when she was not in the presence of the Okusama. And so, almost unobserved by the master of the geisha-house, Moonlight came to the years of maidenhood.

One night the House of Slender Pines was honored by the unexpected advent of most exalted guests. The chief geishas were absent at an entertainment, and Matsuda was in despair. He was forced, consequently, to put the novices into service, and while he bit his nails frenziedly at the awkward movements of the apprentices, Moonlight slipped to his side and whispered in his ear that she was competent to dance as beautifully as the chief geishas. As he stared at her in wrathful irritation, his wife glided to his other side and joined the girl in pleading. Gruffly he consented. Matters could not be much worse. What mattered it now? He was already disgraced in the eyes of the most high. Well, then, let this pet apprentice do her foolish dance.

Moonlight seized her opportunity with the gay avidity of the gambler who tosses his all upon a final chance. At the risk of meeting the fearful displeasure of her master, the ridicule, disdain, and even hatred of the older geishas, whom it was her duty to imitate, the girl danced before the most critical audience in Kioto.

Her triumph was complete. It may have been the novelty or mystery of her dance, the hypnotic perfection of her art; it may have been her own surpassing beauty—no one sought to analyze the source of her peculiar power. Before the smiling, coaxing witchery of her eyes and lips they fell figuratively, and indeed literally, upon their knees.

She became the mad furore and fashion of the hour. Poets indited lyrics to her respective features. Princes flung gifts at her feet. People traveled from the several quarters of the empire to see her. And at this most dangerous period of her career the young Lord Saito Gonji, last of one of the most illustrious families in Japan, crossed her path.

III

His honorable mother declared that Gonji was afflicted with a malady of the stomach. She proffered warm drinks and poultices and sought to induce him to remain in bed. Now that the long and severe years of discipline had passed and her son was at last at home with her, all of the natural mother within her, which had been repressed so long, yearned over her only son. Even her cold and somewhat repelling manner showed a softening.

Had he not been at this time absorbed in his own dreams, Gonji would have met half-way the pathetic advances of his mother; but he was oblivious to the change in her. He insisted politely that his health was excellent, begged to be excused, and wandered off by himself.

His father, whose mighty business interests were in Tokio, abandoned them for the time being and remained by his son's side in Kioto, following the young man assiduously, seeking vainly to arouse him from the melancholy lethargy into which he had fallen. Deep in the heart of the elder Lord Saito was the acute knowledge of what troubled his son, for afflicted he undoubtedly was, as all the relatives unanimously and officiously averred. Such a funereal countenance was unbefitting a bridegroom. One would think the unhappy youth was being driven to his tomb, rather than to the bridal bed!

The parents and relatives vied with each other in importuning the unfortunate Gonji, and sought to distract him from what were evidently his own morbid thoughts. Also they sought to entrap his confidence. Gonji kept his counsel, and from day to day he grew paler, thinner, more silent, and sad.

"Call in the services of the mightiest of honorable physicians and surgeons," ordered the Lady Saito. "It may be an operation will relieve our son."

Her husband, thoughtful, sad, a prey to an uneasy conscience, shook his head dumbly.

"It is not possible for the honorable knife to efface a cancer of the heart," said he, sighing.

"Hasten the nuptials," suggested the uncle of Ohano. "There is no medicine which acts with as drastic force as a wife."

This time the Lord Saito Ichigo was even more emphatic in negativing the suggestion.

"There is time enough," he asserted, gruffly. "I will not begrudge my son at least the short and precious time which should precede the ceremony. This is his period of diversion. It shall not be cut in half."

The brusque words of the head of the Saito house aroused the ire of the nearest relative of the bride. He said complainingly:

"It does not seem as if the honorable bridegroom desires to avail himself of his prenuptial privileges. He does not seek the usual diversions of youth at this time. Is it not unnatural to prefer solitude?"

"It is a matter of choice," contended the father of Gonji, with curt pride.

"But if it injure his health, is it not the duty of the relatives to assist him?"

"The gates of the saito are wide open. My son is not a prisoner. He is at liberty to go whithersoever he pleases. It is apparent that his pleasures lie not outside the ancestral home of his fathers."

"That," said the uncle of Ohano, suavely, "is because he still stumbles in the period of adolescence. It is necessary he be instructed."

The father of Gonji pondered the matter somberly, pulling with thumb and forefinger at his lower lip. After a moment he said, with sudden determination:

"You are right, Takedo Isami. Your superior suggestion is gratefully received. Since my son will not seek the pleasures of youth, let us bring them to our house. It is necessary immediately to arouse him from a youthful despair which may tend to injure his health."

He looked up and met the cunning eye of his prospective kinsman regarding him with a peculiar expression. Ichigo added, gruffly but sturdily:

"It would be an excellent programme to secure the services of the honorable Spider of the House of Slender Pines. I pray you undertake the matter for me. See Matsuda, the master of the house. Spare no expense in the matter."

The expression on Takedo's face was now enigmatic. He emptied his pipe slowly and with deliberation, as if in thought. Then solemnly he bobbed his bald head, as if in assent. The two old men then arose, shaking their skirts and hissing perfunctorily. Their bows were formal, and the words of parting the usual friendly and polite ones; but each met the eye of the other, and both understood; and, strangely, a sense of antagonism arose between them.

IV

S o it was in the honorable house of his father, and of the hundred august ancestors whom they accused him of dishonoring, that Gonji again saw the Spider.

Into the houses of the most exalted the geisha flutters with the free familiarity of a pampered house pet. No festivity, however private, is considered complete without her. She is as necessary as the flowers that bedeck the house, the viands, and the sake.

Upon a humid night in the season of greatest heat, and in the glow of a thousand fireflies, the Spider danced in the gardens of the house of Saito. Her kimono was vermilion, embroidered with dragons of gold. Gold too were her obi and her fan, and red and gold were the ornaments that glistened like fire in her hair. Yet more brilliant, more sparklingly, gleamed and shone the eyes of the dancer, and her scarlet lips were redder than the poppies in her hair, and held an hypnotic allure for the Lord Saito Gonji, watching her in a breathless silence that fairly pained him.

Every gesture, every slightest flutter of her sleeve, her hand, her fan, every smallest turn or motion of her bewitching head, was directed at the guest of honor, the son and heir of the house of Saito. For him alone she seemed to dance. To him she threw her joyous smiles, and, in the end, when the dance was done, it was at his feet she knelt, raising her naïvely coy, half-questioning glance. Then, very softly and with gentle solicitation:

"At your sole honorable service, noble lord," she said. "What is your pleasure next?"

He said, like one awakening from some strange dream or trance:

"It is my pleasure, geisha, that you look into my eyes."

She glanced up timidly, as if troubled and surprised. A wistfully joyous light came into her dark eyes; then they remained unmovingly fixed upon his. Very softly, that those about them might not hear, he whispered:

"I saw your face dimly in the firefly-light. I was possessed with but one ambition—to look into your eyes!"

Her pretty head drooped so low that now it touched his knee. At the contact he trembled and drew sharply away from her. Alarmed, fearing she had unwittingly offended him, she raised her head and looked at him with a mutely questioning glance. There was a cloud, dark and very melancholy, upon the face of the one she had been ordered to entertain. She thought of the instructions of Matsuda: that it should be her paramount duty to beguile and distract the Lord Saito Gonji. Her fortune for life might be made by succeeding in arousing him to a joyous mood. But, lo! the one she sought to please drew back from her, gloomy, troubled.

Her rapid rise to fame had not brought to the Spider the peculiar joy she had anticipated. Fame carries ever with it its bitter savor, and, although she had not alone become the darling of the celebrated geisha-house, but had brought fame and fortune to her master, many of the things she had most cared for she had been obliged to forego in her new position as star of the House of Slender Pines.

No longer was it possible for her to be shielded by the loving arms of the Okusama. Out into the broadest limelight even the delighted Okusama had pushed her, and this blinding light entailed a thousand duties of which she had only vaguely heard from the patronizing elder geishas. She had ceased to be the cuddled and petted little Moonlight, loved and stroked and tossed about by the geishas, because of her beauty and ingenuous wit. Suddenly she had become the Spider! It was a new and fearful name that terrified her.

Matsuda, proud of her success, and at last completely won over, surrounded her with every luxury. So far he had forced upon the girl none of the odious exactions often demanded of the geishas by their masters, even though the law had defined the exact services to which he was legally entitled.

A thousand lovers a geisha might have, said the unwritten law, but to possess one alone was fatal! She must place a guard of iron before her heart! A geisha must sip at love as the bee culls the honey from the blossom, lingering but a moment over each. The rivers and the many pits of death were filled with the bodies of the hapless ones who had gone outside this law, who had dared to permit the passionate heart to escape beyond the prescribed bounds.

Moonlight, with all the witching arts of the geisha at her finger-tips, with a beauty as rare and mysterious as though she were a princess of some new world, had found it thus far an easy task to follow the rules laid down for her class. Like a fragile flower that must not be touched lest its bloom be soiled, the master of the geisha-house jealously protected his star from all possible contamination. She was held out as a lure to captivate and draw to his house the rich and noble ones; but, like some precious jewel in a casket, she was but to be seen, not touched! Matsuda was determined to save his most precious possession for the highest of bidders. Now his patience had met its due reward. The most illustrious head of the house of the exalted Saito solicited his services!

So, while Matsuda gloated over the rich reward to be reaped surely from his lordly patron, the Spider was looking with frightened eyes into those of the Lord Saito Gonji, and she trembled and turned very pale under his somber glance. All her gay insouciance, her saucy, quick repartee, the teasing, witching little graces for which she now was noted, seemed to have deserted her. It troubled her that she was unable to obey the command of her master and make his most noble patron smile. Within the piercing eyes which sought her own she seemed to read only some tragic question, which, alas, she felt unable to answer.

"I desire to please you, noble sir," she said, plaintively, and added, with an impulsive motion of her little hands: "Alas! It is my duty!"

For the first time a faint smile quivered across the young man's lips; but he did not speak. He continued to regard her in that musing fashion, as though he studied every feature of her face and drank in its loveliness with something of resignation and despair.

His curious silence affected her. Was it not possible to arouse the strange one, then, to some animation and interest? Timidly she put out her hand—a mute, charming little gesture—then rested it upon his own. As though her touch had some electric power which stirred him to the depths, he leaned suddenly toward her, inclosing her hand in a close, almost painful grip. Now hungrily, pleadingly, his look enveloped her. His voice trembled with the emotion he sought vainly to control.

"Geisha, if it were possible—if we belonged in another land—if it were not for the customs of the ancestors—I would tell you what is in my heart!"

Like a child, wondering and curious, she answered:

"I pray you, tell me! To keep a troubled secret is like carrying a cup brim full!"

"I will ask you a question," he said incisively. "Wilt thou be my wife for all the lives yet to come?"

As he spoke the forbidden words the Spider turned very pale. She sought to withdraw her trembling hands from his, but he held to them with a passionate tenacity. She could not speak. She could but look at him mutely, piteously; and her lovely, pleading gaze but added to the man's distraction.

"Answer me!" he entreated. "Make me the promise, beautiful little mousmé!"

His vehemence and passion frightened her. She tried to avert her face, to turn it aside from his burning gaze; but he brought his own insistently close to hers. She could not escape his impelling eyes. At last, her bosom heaving up and down like a little troubled sea, she stammered:

"You speak so strangely, noble sir. I—I—am but—a geisha of the House of Slender Pines. Thou art as far above my sphere as—as—are the honorable stars in the heavens."

Her voice had a quality of exquisite terror, as though she sought vainly to thrust aside some hypnotic force to which she yearned to yield. It aroused but the ardor of her lover.

"It is not possible," he murmured, "for one to be above thee, little geisha. Thou art lovelier than all the visions of the esteemed Sun Lady herself. I am thy lover for all time. I desire to possess thee utterly in all the lives yet to come. Make me the promise, beautiful mousmé, that thou wilt travel with me—that thou wilt be mine, mine only!"

She drew back as far from him as it was possible, with her hands jealously held by his own. Her wide, frightened eyes were fixed in terror upon his.

"I cannot speak the words!" she gasped. "I dare not speak them, august one!"

For a moment his face, which had been lighted by excitement and passion, darkened.

"You cannot then return my love?"

"Ah! They are not words for a geisha to speak. It is not for such as I to make the long journey with one so illustrious as thou!"

A sob broke from her, and because she could no longer bear to meet his burning gaze she hid her face with the motion of a child against their clasped hands.

For a long moment there was silence between them. Louder, noisier, rose the mirth of the revelers about them. A dozen geishas pulled at the three-stringed instruments. As many more swayed and moved in the figures of the classical dance. Like great, gaudy butterflies, their bright wings fluttering behind them, the moving figures of the tea-maidens passed before them. Almost it seemed as if they two had been purposely set apart and forgotten. No one approached them. With concerted caution, all avoided a glance in the direction of the guest of honor and the famous one who had been chosen to beguile and save him. How well she had performed her task one could see in the beaming face of Matsuda, the uneasy face of the elder Lord Saito, and the somewhat scowling one of the uncle of Ohano.

The Lord Gonji saw nothing of the relatives. He was oblivious indeed of everything save the shining, drooped little head upon his hands. Scarcely he knew his own voice, so superlatively gentle and wooing was its tone.

"I pray you, give me complete happiness with the promise, beloved one," he entreated.

She raised her head slowly; and gravely, wistfully, her eyes now questioned him. Dimly she realized the effect of such a union upon his haughty family and the ancestors.

She was but a geisha, a cultivated toy, educated for the one purpose of beguiling men and making their lot brighter. Like the painted and grotesque comedian who tortured his limbs to make others laugh, so it was the duty of a geisha to keep ever the laugh upon her lips, even though the heart within her broke. It was not possible that to her, a mere dancing girl, one was offering the entrancing opportunity of which lovers whisper to each other. Her face was very pinched and white, the eyes startlingly large, as she answered him:

"I dare not speak the words, noble sir. I do not know the way. The Meido is very far off. We meet but once. Your honorable parents and the ancestors would turn back one so humble and insignificant as I."

"The honorable parents," he gently explained, "can but point our duty in the present life. In the lives yet to come we choose our own companions. If I could—if it were possible—how gladly would I take thee also for this present life."

She drew back, puzzled, vaguely distressed.

"You—you do not wish me *now* also?" she stammered, and there was a shocked, dazed note in her voice. He saw what was in her mind, and it startled him.

"Do you not know why they have summoned you here to-night?" he questioned.

"At—at the command of my master," she faltered. "I am here to—to please thee, noble sir. If it please thee to make a jest—"

ONOTO WATANNA

She broke off piteously and tried to smile. Her hands slipped from his as he arose suddenly and looked down at her solemnly, where she still knelt at his feet.

"You are here," he said, "to celebrate my honorable betrothal to Takedo Ohano-san."

She did not move, but continued to stare up at him with the dumb-stricken look of one unjustly punished. Then suddenly she sobbed, and her little head rested upon the ground at his feet.

"Geisha!" He called to her sharply, commandingly, and yet with a world of pleading emotion. Matsuda, hovering near, turned and looked loweringly at the girl on the ground. Her face was humbly in the dust at the feet of the Lord Saito Gonji. It was a position unworthy of a geisha, and Matsuda moved furiously nearer to them. This was the work of the Okusama, inwardly he fumed. Now when the geisha was put to the greatest test she was found wanting. At the feet of the man when he should have knelt at hers.

"Geisha!"

This time there was nothing but tenderness in his voice. He was conscious of the fact that the girl at his feet was suffering. He loved her, and was sure that life without her would be both intolerable and worthless. He had begged her to travel with him upon the final "long journey." She, in her simple innocence, believed he had asked her in marriage for this life also. Now, humiliated, she dared not look at him.

Down he knelt beside her; but when he sought to put his arms about her, she sprang wildly to her feet. Not for a moment did she pause, but like some hunted, terrified thing fled fleetly across the garden.

He started to follow, but stopped suddenly, blinded by the sudden excess of madness and rage that swept over him. For, as she ran, her master, Matsuda, doubled over in her path. His face was purple. His wicked little eyes glittered like one gone insane, and his great thick lips fell apart, showing the teeth like tusks of some wild beast. Gonji saw the shining doubled fists as they rose in the air and descended upon the head of the hapless Spider. Then he sprang forward like a madman, leaping at the throat of Matsuda and tossing him aside like some unclean thing.

She lay unmoving upon her back, her arms cast out like the wings of a bird on either side. Gonji caught her up in his arms with a cry that rang out weirdly over the gardens. It stopped the mirth of the revelers and brought them in a hushed group about the pair. Now silence reigned in the gardens of the Saito.

On the upper floor of the mansion the walls had been pushed entirely out so that an open pavilion, flower-laden, made a charming retreat for the "honorable interiors," the ladies of the family, who might not, with propriety, join their lords in the revelry. Here, unseen, these "precious jewels of the household" might watch the celebration; but it was the part of the geisha to entertain their lord. Theirs the lot to receive him when, weary and worn, he must eventually return for rest.

Now, from their sake-sipping the ladies were aroused by that cry of Saito Gonji. Over the lantern-hung, flower-laden trellis they leaned, their shrill voices sounding strangely in the silence that had fallen upon the entire company. Some one lighted a torch and swung it above the group on the ground. Under its light the mother of Gonji, and his bride, Ohano, saw the form of the Spider; and beside her, enveloping her in his arms, whispering to and caressing her, was the Lord Saito Gonji.

Japanese women are trained to hide their deepest emotions. All the world tells of their impassive stoicism; but human nature is human nature, after all. So the bride shrieked like one who has lost his mind, but the cry was strangled ere it was half uttered. When the Lady Saito's hand was withdrawn from the mouth of the bride, the pallid-faced Ohano slipped humbly to her knees, and, shaking like a leaf in a storm, stammered:

"I—I—b-but laughed at the antics of the comedians. Oh, d-d-d-did you see—"

Here she broke off and hid her face, with a muffled sob, upon the breast of the elder woman. Without a word the latter led the girl inside, and the maidens drew the shoji into place, closing the floor.

V

Omi! Omi! Are you there? Wretched little maiden, why do you not come?" The Spider peered vainly down through the patch in her floor. Then, at the faint sound of a sliding foot without, she slapped the section of matting into place again and fell to work in panic haste upon her embroidery.

A passing geisha thrust in a curious face through the screens and wished her a pleasant day's work. The Spider responded cheerfully and showed her little white teeth in the smile her associates knew so well. But the instant the geisha had glided out of sight she was back at the patch again. She called in a whisper: "Omi! Omi! Omi-san!" but no answering treble child-voice responded.

For a while she crouched over the patch and sought to peer down into the passage below. As she knelt, something sharp flew up and smote against her cheek. She grasped at it. Then, hastily closing the patch and, with stealthy looks about her, pausing a moment with alert ears to listen, she opened at last the note. It was crushed about a pebble, and was written on the thinnest of tissue-paper.

Moonlight drank in avidly the burning words of love in the poem. Her eyes were shining and brilliant, her cheeks and lips as red as the poppies in her hair, when Matsuda thrust back the sliding screens and entered the chamber. He said nothing to the smiling geisha, but contented himself with scrutinizing her in a calculating manner, as though he summarized her exact value. Then, with a jerk or nod apparently of satisfaction, he left the room, and the girl was enabled to reread the beloved epistle.

A few moments later the screens which Matsuda had carefully closed behind him were cautiously parted a space, and the thin, impish, pert, and precocious face of a little girl of thirteen was thrust in. She made motions with her lips to the Spider, who laughed and nodded her head.

Omi—for it was she—slipped into the room. She was an odd-looking little creature, her body as thin as her wise little face, above which her hair was piled in elaborate imitation of the coiffure of her mistress and preceptress. She fell to work at once, solicitously arranging the dress and hair of the Spider and complaining bitterly that the maids had neglected, shamefully, her beloved mistress's toilet.

"Although it is not the proper work for an apprentice-geisha," she rattled along, "yet I myself will serve your honorable body, rather than permit it to suffer from such pernicious neglect."

She smoothed the little hands of her mistress, manicured and perfumed them, talking volubly all the time upon every subject save the one the Spider was waiting to hear about. At last, unable to bear it longer, Moonlight broke in abruptly:

"How you chatter of insignificant matters! You tease me, Omi. I shall have to chastise you. Tell me in a breath about the matter."

Omi grinned impishly, but at the reproachful look of her mistress her natural impulse to torment even the one she loved best in the world gave way. She began in a gasp, as though she had just come hastily into the room.

"Oh, oh, you would never, never believe it in the world. Nor could I, indeed, had I not seen it with my own insignificant eyes."

"Yes, yes, speak quickly!" urged the Spider, eagerly hanging upon the words of the apprentice.

Omi drew in and expelled her breath in long, sibilant hisses after the manner of the most exalted of aristocrats.

"There are six of them at the gates, not to count the servants and runners down the road!"

Moonlight looked at her incredulously, and Omi nodded her head with vigor.

"It is so. I counted each augustness." She began enumerating upon her fingers. "There was the high-up Count Takedo Isami, Takedo Sachi, Takedo—there were four Takedos. Then the Lord Saito Takamura Ichigo, Saito—"

"Do not enumerate them, Omi. Tell me instead how you came, in spite of the watchful ones, in spite, too, of Matsuda, to reach his lordship."

As she spoke the last word reverently, a flush deepened in her cheeks and her eyes shone upon the apprentice with such a lovely light that the adoring little girl cried out sharply:

"It is true, Moonlight-san! Thou art lovelier than Ama-terasu-o-mi-kami!"

"Hush, foolish one, that is blasphemy. Indeed I should be very unhappy did I outshine the august lady of the sun in beauty. But no more digressions. If you do not tell me—and tell me at once—exactly what happened—how you reached the side of his lordship—how he looked—just how! What was said—the very words—how he spoke—acted. Did he smile, or was he sad, Omi? Tell me—tell me, please!" She ended coaxingly; but, as the pert little apprentice merely smiled tantalizingly, she added, very severely:

"It may be I will look about for a new understudy. There is Ochika—"

At the mention of her rival's name Omi made a scornful grimace, but she answered quickly:

"The Okusama helped me. She pretended an illness. Matsuda was afraid, and remained by her side, chafing her hands and her head." She laughed maliciously, and continued: "I slipped out by the bamboo-hedge gate. Omatsu saw me—" At the look of alarm on the Spider's face: "Pooh! what does it matter? Every servant in the house—ah! and the maids and apprentices—yes, and the most honorable geishas too—know the secret, and they wish you well, sweet mistress!"

She squeezed Moonlight's hands with girlish fervor, and the latter returned the pressure lovingly, but besought her to continue.

"The main gates were closed. Just think! No one is admitted even to the gardens. Why, 'tis like the days of feudalism. We are in a fortress, with the enemy on all sides!"

"Oh, Omi, you let your imagination run away with you, and I hang upon your words, waiting to hear what has actually happened."

"I am telling you. It is exactly as I have said. Matsuda dares not offend the powerful family of the Saito, and it is at their command that the gates of the House of Slender Pines are closed rigorously to all the public. No one dare enter. No one dare—go out—save—I!" and she smiled impudently. "It is said"—lowering her voice confidentially—"that Matsuda has been paid a vast sum of 'cash' to keep his house closed. Mistress, there are great notices in black and white nailed upon the line of trees clear down the road. 'The House of Slender Pines is closed for the season of greatest heat!' And just think," and the little apprentice-geisha pouted, "not a koto or a samisen is permitted to be touched! Who ever heard of a geisha-house as silent as a mortuary hall? It is very sad. We wish to sing and dance and court the smiles of noble gentlemen; but you have made such a mess with your honorable love affair that every geisha and every apprentice is being punished! We are not permitted to speak above a whisper. Our lovers must stand beyond the gates and serenade us themselves. It is—"

"Oh, Omi, you wander so! Now tell me, sweet girl, exactly what I am perishing to know."

"I will, duly! You preach patience to me so often," declared the impish little creature; "now you must practise it also. I resume my narrative. Pray do not interrupt so often, as it delays my story." With that she leisurely proceeded.

"Mistress, the entire gardens of the House of Slender Pines are *patrolled*—yes, and by armed samourai!"

"Samourai! You speak nonsense. There is no such thing to-day as a samourai. Swords, moreover, are not permitted. Omi, you are tormenting me, and it is very unkind and ungrateful. You will force me to punish you very severely, much as I love you!"

"It is as I have said. I speak only the truth. The ones who guard our house are exalted ones—samourai by birth at least, relatives of his lordship. They do not permit even the smallest aperture to be unwatched, whereby his lordship might slip into the gardens, and from thence into my mistress's chamber—"

"Omi!"

"—for it has gone abroad through all the Saito clan that the peace of the most honorable ancestors is about to be imperiled."

Moonlight's color was dying down, and as the little girl proceeded her two hands stole to her breast and clung to where the love poem was hidden.

"As the relatives cannot by entreaty force his lordship from your vicinity, loveliest of mistresses, they are bent upon guarding him, in case by the artful intrigues known only to lovers"—and the little maiden shook her head with precocious wisdom—"he may actually reach your side despite the care of Matsuda."

Moonlight now seemed scarcely to be listening. She was looking out dreamily before her, and her fancy conjured up the inspired face of her lover. She felt again the warm touch of his lips against her hair, and heard the ardent, passionate promise he had made in the little interval when she had come to consciousness within his arms there in the gardens of his ancestors. "If it is impossible to have you—ay, in this very life—then I will wed no other. No! though the voices of all the ancestors shout to me to do my duty!"

Now she knew he was very near to her. For days they had been unable to induce him to leave the vicinity of her home. Outside the gates of the closed geisha-house he had taken his stand, there to importune the implacable Matsuda and try vainly, by every ruse and device, to reach her side.

Though she knew that never for a moment would the watchful relatives permit him to be alone, still at last he had eluded them sufficiently to send her word through the clever little Omi. Now she listened with tingling ears, as Omi glibly and with exaggeration told how, as she flew by on her skipping-rope, he had slipped the note into her sleeve. Only this acute child could have outwitted Matsuda in this way. A few moments of hiding in the deserted ozashiki, a chance to toss the note aloft to her mistress, and then to await her opportunity when the lower halls should be clear and slip upstairs! Apprentices were not permitted to be thus at large, and Omi knew that, if caught, her punishment would be quite dreadful; but she gaily took the risk for her beloved mistress.

She sat back now on her heels, having finished her recital. She watched Moonlight, as the latter read and reread her love missive. Much to the disappointment of the little maiden, her mistress did not read it aloud. The sulky pout, however, soon faded from the girl's lips, as her mistress put her cheek against Omi's thin little one. With arms enclasped, the two sat in silence, watching the falling of the twilight; and in the mind of each one solitary figure stood clearly outlined. His features were delicate, his arched eyebrows as sensitive as a poet's, his lips as full and pouting as a child's. His eyes were large and long and somewhat melancholy, but there were latent hints within them of a stronger power capable of awakening. Upon his face was that ineffaceable stamp of caste, and it lent a charm to the youth's entire bearing.

A maid pattered into the apartment and lit the solitary andon. Its wan light added but a feeble gleam in the darkened room. Presently she returned, bearing the simple meal for the geisha and her apprentice. When this was finished, with the aid of Omi she spread the sleeping-quilts and snuffed the andon light. It was the orders of Matsuda that the house should be darkened at the hour when previously it was lighted most gaily. There was nothing left for them to do save go to bed. Yet for some time, in the darkened chamber, with its closed walls, the two remained whispering and planning; and once the watchful maid upon her sleeping-mat outside the screens heard the soft, musical laughter of the famous geisha, and the servant sighed uneasily. She did not like this work assigned her by Matsuda.

In the middle of the night Omi, turning on the quilts, missed her mistress at her side. Arising, she felt along the floor beside her.

Then, alarmed, she slipped out from under the netting. It was a clear moonlight night, and a golden stream came into the room through the widely opened shoji. Leaning against it, with her dreamy head resting upon the trellis, was her mistress. By the light of the moon she held the shimmering sheets of tissue-paper, and over these she still pored and wept.

VI

O f the once flourishing and numerous family of the Saito, there were but two male members living, Saito Gonji, and his father, Saito Ichigo. The relatives of the Lady Saito were, however, numerous, and, like the mother of Gonji, they possessed stern and domineering dispositions. In contrast, her husband was easy-going and genial, and it had been an easy matter, in consequence, thus far, for the relatives to rule the head of the illustrious house. Lord Ichigo had even followed their counsel in the matter of the education of his boy, although it had cut him to the heart to resign his cherished son at so tender an age to the severe tutors chosen for him by his wife's relatives.

When Ohano had been selected as a wife for the youth, the father of Gonji had offered no objection. In fact, there was little that he could have found to object to in this particular matter. The girl was of a family equally honorable; her health was excellent; she had shown no traits of character objectionable in a woman. Indeed, she appeared to be an honorable and desirable vehicle to hand down the race of Saito of imperishable fame. And that, of course, was the main idea of marriage. It was a matter of duty to the ancestors, and not of desire of the individuals. So the peace-loving elder Lord Saito believed, at the time of the betrothal, that he had safely disposed of a most vexing problem.

He was dumbfounded, panic-stricken, at the turn events had taken. On all sides, harangued by that insistent lady, his wife, and also by her many relatives, he found it, nevertheless, impossible to turn a deaf ear to the impassioned pleading of the young man himself. Day and night Gonji desperately beset his father, ignoring utterly all other members of the family.

His vigil of many days before the gates of the House of Slender Pines had but strengthened the young man's resolve. At any cost—yes, at the sacrifice of the ancestors' honor even—he was determined to possess the Spider. Since he was assured that his passion was returned—and the assurance came through the lips of the little Omi, who had screeched the words impishly in his ear, as if in derision, that those about them might not suspect—Gonji determined to marry the geisha not alone in the thousand vague lives yet to come, but in the present one, too. He must have her now. It was impossible to wait, he told his father. If the cruel laws forbade their union, then they would go to the gods, and the less harsh heart of the river would receive them in a bridal night that would never pass away.

It is not an easy matter for a youth in Japan to marry without the full consent of his parents. Every possible obstacle had been thrown into the path of the despairing Gonji. Even his revenue was cut off completely, so that, even had he been able to move the stony heart of the geisha-keeper from the position he had taken at the behest of the powerful family, Gonji had not the means to purchase the girl's freedom from her bonds. There was nothing, therefore, left for the unfortunate Gonji save to focus all his energies upon his father; and day and night he besieged the unhappy Ichigo.

The latter had listened, without comment, to the law as laid down by Takedo Isami, the uncle of Ohano. He had listened to the urgings of the many other relatives of his wife that he remain firm throughout the ordeal they realized he was passing through. He had given an equally attentive ear to the besieging relatives and to the stern Lady Saito, who was confident of the powerful influence of the tongue upon her lord. Then he had hearkened in silence, with drawn, averted face, to the desperate pleading of his only son, the one creature in the world that he truly loved.

While the father miserably debated the matter within himself, Gonji suddenly ceased to importune his parent. Retiring to his own chamber, he closed and fastened the doors against all possible intruders.

The relatives regarded this latest act of their fractious young kinsman as an evidence that at last his impetuous young will was breaking. They congratulated themselves upon their firmness at this time, and advised Lord Saito Ichigo to retain an unbending attitude in the matter.

The abrupt retirement of his son, however, had a strange effect upon Ichigo. He could think of nothing save the youth's last words. He dared not confide his fears even to his wife, who was already sufficiently distracted by her task of caring for Ohano and her anxiety about her son.

Against the advice of the relatives that Gonji be left alone to fight out the battle by himself, his father forced his way into the boy's presence. Gonji responded neither to his knocking nor to his father's imperative call. So Lord Ichigo forced the screens apart.

In one glance the father of Gonji saw what it was the desperate young man now contemplated, for he had robed himself from head to foot in the white garments of the dead. His face was, moreover, as fixed and white as though already he had started upon the journey.

"Gonji—my dear son!"

The elder Lord Saito scarce knew his own voice, so hoarse and full of anguished emotion was it. He stood close by the kneeling Gonji and rested his hands heavily upon the boy's slender shoulders. Gonji looked up slowly and met his father's gaze. A mist came before his eyes, but he spoke steadily, gently:

"It is better this way. I pray you to pardon me. I am unable to serve the ancestors."

"It is not of the ancestors I think," said Lord Saito, gruffly, "but of you—you only, my son!"

Gonji looked at him strangely now, as though he sought to fathom the mind of his father; but he turned away, perplexed and distressed.

"You must believe that," went on his father, brokenly. "What is best for your happiness, that is my wish, above all things. If happiness is only possible for you by giving you what is your heart's desire, then"—a smile broke over the grave, pain-racked features of his father, as though a weight were suddenly lifted from his heart at the sudden resolve that had come to him—"then," he continued, "it shall be!"

With a cry, Gonji gripped at his parent's hands, his eyes turned imploringly upon Lord Saito's face.

"You mean—ah, you promise, then—" He could not speak the words that rushed in a flood to his lips.

"Hé! (Yes!)" said Lord Ichigo, solemnly. "It is a promise."

VII

Having determined upon the course to take, Lord Saito Ichigo summoned a council of the relatives of the family.

For the first time, possibly, since his marriage, he faced the assembled kinsfolk with the calm demeanor of one who had seized, and intended to retain, the authority properly invested in him as head of the house of Saito. His should be the voice heard! His the decision that must prevail!

In the minds of most men—Japanese men, at least—who have married at the dictates of their parents, there is always some little cherished chamber to which, despite the passing years, memory returns with loving, loitering step. So with Lord Ichigo. Now, with the fate of his beloved child in his hands, the father looked back upon his own life, and it was no reflection upon his excellent and virtuous wife that he did so with just a shade of vague regret.

The impetuous Gonji's passionate words had not been spoken to deaf ears. Lord Saito Ichigo was determined to keep his promise to his son, whatever the result; for well he knew of the upheaval in his household which would be sure to follow.

There was, of course, Ohano to think of. Her case was not as difficult as it seemed, he pointed out to the assembled relatives. An orphan, one of a family already allied by marriage to the Saitos, they had taken her into their house at an early age. They already regarded her as a daughter. As for a daughter, they would seek, outside their own family, for a worthy and suitable husband for the maiden. In fact, it was better that Ohano should marry another than Lord Gonji, since the latter had always looked upon her as a sister, and a union between them was, to him, repugnant. That, indeed, Ichigo himself had thought at first, but he had desired to please "the honorable interior" (his wife) and the many relatives of his honorable wife.

Thus he disposed of this matter briefly, and, although the relatives looked at each other with startled glances, they had nothing to say. Something in the fixed attitude of the one they had hitherto somewhat contemptuously regarded as weak and yielding claimed now their respectful attention.

To approach the matter of the marriage of a Saito with a public geisha required not alone tact, but bravery. Hardly had the father of Gonji mentioned the matter when a storm of dissent arose. To a man—to say nothing of the countless unseen female relatives arrayed even more bitterly against her—the exalted kinsmen resented even the suggestion of such a union. So the Lord Ichigo approached the subject by wary paths.

In the first place, he pointed out boldly, the assembled ones were not actually of the Saito blood, but relatives by marriage only; and, while their counsel and advice were respectfully and gratefully solicited, even their united verdict could not finally stand out against the legal head of the house. This bold statement at the outset met a silence more eloquent of resentment than any storm of words.

It was imperative, as all had agreed, continued Lord Ichigo, that the son and heir of the house of Saito should make an early marriage. He was the last of the line. The glorious and heroic ancestors demanded descendants. It was a sacred duty to keep alive the illustrious seed.

Lord Ichigo launched into a detailed recital here of the notable deeds of his ancestors, but was stopped abruptly by the sarcastic comment of Takedo Isami, who quoted the ancient proverb, "There is no seed to a great man!" meaning none could inherit his greatness.

This cut off Ichigo's oratory; and, hurt and disturbed at the quotation as a reflection upon his own shortcomings, he brought up squarely before them the main issue.

These were the days of enlightenment, when the iron-clad ships of war sailed the seas as far as the great Western lands; when the Japanese had accepted the best of the ways of the West; when the spirit of the New Japan permeated every nook and corner of the empire. There was one Western privilege which the men of New Japan were now demanding, and desired above all things. That they must have: the right to love!

Now, "love" is not a very proper word, according to the Japanese notion of polite speech. Hence the attitude of the relatives. Nor did the frigid atmosphere melt in the slightest before the flow of fervid eloquence that the father of Gonji brought to the defense of this reprehensible weakness.

Takedo Isami, who seemed to have assumed the position of leader and dictator among the relatives, arose slowly to his feet, and, thrusting out a pugnacious chin, asked for the right to speak. He was short, dark, with the face of a fighter and the body of a dwarf.

Admitting the right of man to love, he said it was better to hide this weakness, and, by all means, fight its insidious effort to enter the household. Only men of low morals married for love. Duty was so beautiful a thing that it brought its own reward. The proper kind of love—the lofty and the pure—declared the uncle of Ohano, came always after marriage, and sanctified the union. That the last of a great race, in whose keeping the ancestors had confidently placed the family honor, should contemplate a union of mere love and passion with a notorious and public geisha was a gratuitous and cruel insult not alone to his many living relatives—and they of his mother's side were equally of his blood—but to the ancestors.

As the uncle of Ohano reseated himself a low murmur of approbation broke out from the circle. Gloomy looks were turned toward Ichigo, whose face had become curiously fixed. Far from weakening his resolve, his pride had been stung to the quick. Nothing, he told himself inwardly, would cause him to retreat from the position he had taken. He looked Takedo Isami squarely in the eye ere he spoke.

The honorable Takedo Isami's remarks, he declared, were a reflection upon his own, since they concerned one whom the ancestors and the Lord Saito Gonji deemed worthy to honor. Moreover, it was both vain and reprehensible to cast a stone at a profession honored by all intelligent Japanese. It was of established knowledge that often the geishas were recruited from the noblest families in Japan. It was absurd to regard them with disdain, as apparently had latterly become the fashion. There was no great event in the history of the nation since feudal times wherein the geisha had not played her part nobly. The greatest of sacrifices she had made for her country and the Mikado. There were instances, too famous to need repeating, of the most exquisite martyrdom. The Emperor, the nobility, the priests—all delighted to do her honor. Only the ignorant assumed to despise her. She was in reality the darling and the pride of the entire nation. One would as soon dream of being without the flowers and the birds, and all the other joyous things of life, as the geisha. Who was it, then, dared to reflect upon the most charming of Japanese institutions?

Up sprang Takedo Isami, his hand raised, his dark face flushed with fury, despite the restraint he sought to exercise upon his features. His voice was under control, and he spoke with incisive bitterness.

His honorable kinsman, he loudly declared, wished but to confuse the issue. No one denied the virtues of the geisha; also the undoubted fact that many of them came from the impoverished families of the samourai. Nevertheless, charming and desirable as she was, she had not been educated to be the mother of a great race. Her lithe, twisting, dancing little body was not meant to bear children. Her light, frivolous mind was ill-fitted to instruct one's sons and daughters. Society had set her in her proper place. It was against all precedents to take her from her sphere. One did not desire as a mate through life a creature of mere beauty, any more than one would care to take one's daily bowl of rice from a fragile work of art which would shatter at the mere contact of the sturdy chop-sticks against it.

Such a storm of dissent and discussion now arose that it was impossible for the father of Gonji to hear his own voice, and indeed all seemed to make an effort to drown it. So he summoned servants, and coolly bade them put the amado (outside sliding walls) in place, lest the unseemly noise of wordy strife be heard by some passing neighbor— for the Japanese esteem it a disgrace to engage in controversy. Then, when the doors were in place, Lord Saito Ichigo gravely bowed to the assembled relatives, and, taking his son by the arm, bade them good night, advising that they argue the matter among themselves, without his unnecessary presence.

VIII

The most dreaded moment of a Japanese girl's life is when she enters the house of the mother-in-law. Her future happiness, she knows, is in the hands of this autocratic and all-powerful lady. Meekly the wise bride enters, with propitiating smiles and gifts, robed in her most inconspicuous gown, her aim being not to enhance whatever beauty she may possess, but, if possible, to hide it.

Far more necessary is it for her to have the goodwill of the mother-in-law than that of the husband. It is even possible for the mother-in-law, for certain causes, to divorce the young wife. In point of fact, the bride goes on trial not to her husband, but to her husband's parents. It depends entirely upon their verdict whether she shall be "returned" or not. In most cases, however, where the marriage is arranged between the families, there is the desire to please the family of the bride; and it is more often the case than not that the parents of the husband receive the little, fearful bride with open arms and hearts.

The geisha is not educated for marriage. From her earliest years, indeed, she is taught that her office in life is merely to entertain.

In the case of the Spider, she had even less opportunity for knowing the rules that prevailed in such matters. She had been educated by the witless wife of the geisha-keeper. All her short life had been spent in aiding nature to make her more beautiful, more charming. The most important thing in life, the thing that brought rare smiles of admiration to even the sternest lips, was to be beautiful, witty, and charming.

So the Spider set out for the Saito house with a light and fearless heart, confident in the power of her beauty and witchery to win even the most frosty-hearted of mothers-in-law. Arrayed in the most gorgeous robe the geisha-house afforded, with huge flowers in her hair, her little scarlet fan fluttering at her breast, attended by her no less gaudily dressed maiden and apprentice, Omi, and followed almost to the gates of the estate by a procession of well-meaning friends and former comrades, the geisha entered the ancestral home of the illustrious family. For just a moment, ere she entered, she paused upon the threshold, a premonitory thrill of fear seizing her. She clung to the supporting hand of the garrulous Omi, whose shrill and acid little tongue already grew mute in the silent halls of the shiro (mansion).

Presently they were ushered into the ozashiki, and the Spider became conscious of the stiff and ceremonious figures standing back coldly by the screens, their gowns seeming in the subdued light of the room of a similar dull color to the satin fusuma of the walls, their shining topknots undecorated with flower or ornament, their thin, unmoving lips and eyes almost closed in cold, unsmiling scrutiny of the intruder, who seemed, like some brilliant butterfly, to have dropped in their midst from another world.

The women of the household—and these comprised the mother, two austere maternal aunts, and Takedo Ohano-san (she who was to have been the bride of Lord Gonji)—surveyed the Spider with narrow, keen eyes that took in every detail of her flaming gown, her dazzling coiffure, flower-laden, and, beneath, the exquisite little face, with wide and starlit eyes that looked at them now in friendly appeal.

There was no word spoken. Nothing but the sighing, hissing sound of indrawn breaths, as with precise formality they made their obeisances to the bride.

In vain did the wandering eyes of the geisha scan the farthermost corner of the great room in search of her lover, or even his seemingly friendly father. There were only the women there to receive her.

Dimly, now, she recalled hearing or reading somewhere that this was a fashion followed by many families—the reception of the bride at first alone by the women of the house, who were later to present her to the assembled relatives. But why this disconcerting silence? Why the cold, unfriendly, lofty gaze of these unmoving women? They stood like grave automata, regarding sternly the bride of the Lord Saito Gonji.

The smile upon the geisha's lips flickered away tremulously; her little head drooped like a flower; she closed her eyes lest the threatening tears might fall.

A voice, cold, harsh, and with that note of command of one in authority addressing a servant, at last broke the silence.

"It is my wish," said the Lady Saito Ichigo, "that you retire to your chamber, and there remove the garments of your trade."

So strange and unexpected were the words that at first the Spider did not realize that they could possibly be addressed to her. She looked up, bewildered, and encountered the steely gaze of the mother-in-law. Moonlight never forgot that first glance. In the unrelenting gaze bent upon her she read what brought havoc and pain to her heart, for all the stored-up resentment and hatred that burned within the

Lady Saito Ichigo showed now in her face. Her voice droned on with mechanical, incisive calmness, but always with the cruel and harsh tone of contemptuous command:

"It is my wish that your maiden of the geisha-house be returned at once to her proper home."

She clapped her hands precisely twice, and a serving-woman answered the summons and knelt respectfully to take the order of her mistress.

"You will conduct the wife of the Lord Saito Gonji to her chamber."

The servant crossed to the still kneeling Moonlight, and while the latter, mystified, looked dumbly at the exalted but, to her, horrible lady, she assisted the Spider to arise. Mechanically and fearfully, pausing not even at the wrathful, sobbing outcry that had broken loose from Omi, she followed in the wake of the serving-maid.

Presently she found herself in an empty chamber, unlike any she had known in the geisha-house, with its golden matting shining like glass, and its lacquer latticed walls of water-paper, and the sliding screens, rare and exquisite works of art. Here the maid fell to work upon the geisha, removing every vestige of her attire and substituting the plain but elegant flowing robes of a lady of rank.

From the geisha's hair she removed the ornaments and the poppies. She swept it down, like a cloud of lacquer, upon the shoulders of the girl, then drew it up into the stiff and formal mode proper for one of her class. From the girl's face she wiped the last trace of rouge and powder, revealing the rosy, shining skin beneath, clear and clean as a baby's.

When she emerged from the hands of the maid, Moonlight looked at herself curiously in the small mirror tendered her, and for a moment she stared, dumbfounded at the face that looked back at her. It seemed so strangely young, despite its wide and wounded eyes. Though she was in reality more charming than ever, seeming like one who had come from a fresh and invigorating bath, the geisha felt that the last vestige of her beauty had fled. Within her heart arose a panic-stricken fear of the effect of the metamorphosis upon her lord. She wished ardently she were back in the noisy geisha-house, with the maidens clamoring about her and the apprentices vying with one another in imitating her. She put the mirror behind her. Her lips trembled so she could hardly compress them, and to avoid the scrutiny of the maid she moved blindly to the shoji. There she stared out unseeingly at the landscape before her, heroically trying to choke back the tears that would force their way and dripped down her dimpled cheeks like rain.

Some one whispered her name, very softly, adoringly. She turned and looked at him—her young bridegroom, with his pale face alight with happiness. She tried to answer him, but even his name eluded her. It was the first time they had been alone together, the first time they had seen each other since that night in the gardens of the Saito.

"Why, how beautiful thou art!" he stammered. "More so even than I had dreamed!"

He was very close to her now, and almost unconsciously she leaned against him. His arms enfolded her rapturously, and she felt his young cheek warm against her own.

IX

"The mistake—you will admit it was a mistake?—was to have countenanced such a match at all," said the Lady Saito Ichigo.

Her husband's manner was less sure, less unyielding than it had been in many days. Indeed, there was a slightly apologetic tone in his voice, and he avoided the angry eyes of his spouse. He too had seen the arrival of the Spider!

"Well, well, let us admit it, then, for the sake of peace. The marriage was a mistake. But consider, our son's happiness—nay, his very life!—was at stake."

He lowered his voice.

"I will tell you in confidence that which I had discovered. They had already made their plans to marry."

"Pff!" Lady Saito waved the matter aside as unbelievable. "Will you tell me how they were to do this thing? Marriage, fortunately, is not such an easy matter without the consent of the parents. Moreover, the woman was under bonds to her keeper."

"You forget there are other unions possible to lovers. You should know that many such start bravely on the long journey to the Meido when it is impossible to marry in this life."

Lady Saito turned her face slowly toward her husband and fixed him with a piercing, bitter glare.

"That," said Ichigo, gently, "was the union contemplated by our children."

His wife drew in her breath in that peculiar, hissing fashion of the Japanese. Her beady little eyes glittered like fire.

"That was what *she*—the Spider woman—induced my son to do! You see, do you not, how completely she has seduced him—even from his duty to his parents and his ancestors?"

She beat out the minute blaze from her pipe, digging into it with her forefinger. Then, first coughing harshly to attract the attention of the young people, she called out loudly:

"Come hither, if you please! I say, come! You seem to forget you are no longer in the geisha-house. It is the voice of supreme authority which summons you now. A cup of tea, if you please—and water for my honorable feet!"

She repeated the demand twice, in a peremptory voice; and now she arose to her feet and advanced a step almost threateningly toward the young couple.

They had been smiling into each other's eyes. They were oblivious of everything and every one in the room, for they were in that exalted and enraptured condition of first love which makes the individual seem almost stupid and obtuse to all save the loved one. Only dimly the words of their mother had reached them, and they stirred like children rudely awakened from some beautiful dream. The smile was still on the face of the girl as she turned toward her mother-in-law; but it slowly faded, leaving her pale, confused, and timorous. She met the malevolent gaze of the older woman, and began to tremble.

She tried to speak, and her hand reached out flutteringly toward her husband—a charming, helpless little gesture that warmed him to the soul. He inclosed the little reaching hand, and thus, hand in hand, they faced the enraged lady.

"Your manners, my good girl, are in keeping with the geisha-house. Is it the fashion there to ignore the voice of authority?"

The bride's large, dark eyes had widened in innocent surprise. Only partially she seemed to comprehend the older woman's attitude. She had been but a day in the house of the parents-in-law. No one as yet had taught her, the cherished, petted, adored star of the House of Slender Pines, that the position of a daughter-in-law is often as lowly as that of a servant. Not even by Matsuda had she ever been thus offensively addressed. She said, stammeringly:

"I—I—have not heard the voice of which you speak, august lady."

A cruel smile curled the lips of her mother-in-law.

"Then it is time, my girl, that you kept your ears wide open."

She sat down upon her heels abruptly by the hibachi.

"Tea is desirable for the honorable insides. Water for my feet, which are tired!"

The girl's eyes turned inquiringly toward her husband. He had grown darkly red. For a moment he seemed about to speak protestingly to his mother; then in a whisper he murmured to his bride:

"It is your—duty!"

Moonlight's shocked glance had gone from her husband's face to the opposite shoji. There, in dumb show, a maid beckoned to her. Without a word her lovely little head bowed in meek assent; she began upon her first menial task.

When she was gone Gonji looked scowlingly at the back of his mother's head—she had turned her face rigidly from him. He felt keenly the danger threatening his wife, the one he adored. He knew the exact power in the hands of the mother-in-law, the cruel whip of authority it was possible for her to wield. That Moonlight would be forced to succumb to the common lot of many unhappy wives he had not realized. Secretly he determined to help her in every way possible within his power.

"What has come over you?" His mother's voice broke upon his miserable reverie, and it was as harsh as the one she employed to his wife. "Is it a new fashion of the geisha-house perchance—to answer a parent's question with silence?"

"Did you question me, mother? I am sorry I did not hear you."

"Oh, it is of no consequence. Besides, you are not listening, even now. Your eyes are still upon the screen through which the insignificant daughter-in-law passed to do me service."

He flushed and bit his lips. Something in his mother's baleful look moved him to an impetuous cry:

"Mother! Do not hate my wife! If you could but know her as she is, so sweet and lovely and—"

"There is no medicine for a fool!" snarled his mother, enraged at the boy's apparent infatuation.

Moonlight, who had pushed the sliding doors open, heard the words, and now she paused, looking from one to the other. Gonji hastened across to her and seized the pail of water from her hand.

"It is too heavy for hands so small—and so lovely!" he cried, and then, as though aghast at his own words, he again pleadingly faced his mother.

"We have many servants. Why give such employment to my wife?"

"Since when," demanded the mother, hoarsely, "did a childless son become master in his father's house?"

"These are modern times, mother," he protested. "She has not been bred for service such as this!"

"Then it is time we undertook her education," said his mother, ominously. "In the house of the honorable mother-in-law she will quickly learn her proper place."

She put out her feet, and the girl knelt and washed them.

Alone that evening in their room, they clung together like frightened children. It had been a hard, a cruel day for both.

"It is true," she said, searching his face in the hope of finding a denial there, "that your parents bitterly hate me."

"They will outgrow it. It is not so with my father, and later you will win my mother's affection. Your sweetness, beauty, goodness, beloved one, will win her even against her will."

She held him back from her, with her two little hands resting flatly on his breast.

"They despise me because I am a geisha? That is why they treat me so."

"No, it is not that only. It is often the case at first in the house of the parents-in-law. It is your duty to serve them—to obey even their cruel caprices. But"—and he drew her into a warm embrace—"it will not be for long! Maybe a year—longer, if the gods decree it! You can bear it for a little while, can you not, for me?"

"And after that?" she persisted, with the clear-eyed innocence of a child.

"After that? Why, the gods are good!" he cried, joyously. "We will have our own home. The humblest daughter-in-law is elevated with the coming of an heir!"

Her eyes were very wide, and in their dark depths he saw a piteous look of terror there. She caught at his hand and clung to it.

"Gonji! Suppose—suppose it is not possible for me—to please the gods!" she gasped. "Ah!"—as he hastened to reassure her—"it is said by the wise ones that a geisha is but a fragile toy, for transient pleasure only, but with neither the body nor the heart to mother a race!"

X

Life for a young wife in the house of her parents-in-law in Japan is seldom a bed of roses. Of the entire family she is, up to a certain period, the most insignificant. Under the most galling circumstances the Japanese bride remains meek, dutiful, patient. She dare not even look too fondly for comfort from her husband, lest she arouse the jealousy of the august lady, for no woman can, with equanimity, endure the thought that her adored son prefers another to herself.

Moonlight's lot was harder than that of most brides, for, besides the menial tasks assigned her, she was obliged to endure the veiled, insulting references to her former caste, and to carry always with her the knowledge that she was not alone despised but hated by her husband's people.

There was one compensation, however. Far from decreasing, the love of the young Lord Gonji for his beautiful wife grew ever stronger. It was impossible, moreover, for him to conceal the state of his heart from the lynx-eyed, passionately jealous mother, with the consequence that she let no opportunity escape her of making her daughter's life a burden. In this venomous task she was ably assisted by Ohano, who was still a member of the household.

In contrast to the treatment accorded the young wife, Ohano was cherished and made the constant companion and confidante of Lady Saito. Always healthy, plump, and active, she presented at this time a striking contrast to the wistful-eyed and fragile Moonlight, who looked as if a breath might blow her away. She was given to dreaming and star-gazing, a girl devoted to poetry and music. In the geisha-house her fresh, young laughter had mingled at all times with the other joyous sounds. Now, however, she seemed under some spell. She was a different creature, one who even moved uncertainly, starting painfully at the slightest motion and flushing and paling whenever addressed.

She had set herself the task of studying "The Greater Learning for Women," and now, painfully, from day to day, she, who had once gaily ordered all about her, tried to obey meekly the strict rules laid down for her sex by Confucius.

No matter how humiliating the task set her, how harshly, and even cruelly, the tongue of the mother-in-law lashed her, she made no murmur of complaint. But daily she visited the Temple. While it seemed as if her back must break from weariness, she would remain upon her knees for hours at the shrine, murmuring ever one insistent, passionate prayer to the gods.

The first year passed away, and there was no change in the household of the Saitos.

A letter came to the young wife from the wife of Matsuda, entreating her former favorite to come to her for a little visit. The letter was laid meekly before the mother-in-law, and, to the girl's surprise, permission was granted. Her husband took her to her former home and left her there among her friends.

They had both expected that her health would be improved by the change, by the reunion with old friends and comrades, the brightness and cheer of the House of Pleasure, and the throng of admiring maidens and geishas about her. But, instead, the place had a depressing effect upon the former geisha. The lights, the constant strumming of drum and samisen, the singing, the continuous dancing and chatting, bewildered her, and before the week was over she returned to her husband's home. Hardly, however, had she entered the Saito house when a new fear seized her.

Something in the silent, speculating gaze of her mother-in-law smote her heart with terror. Of what was the older woman thinking, she wondered, and what had put that curious smile of satisfied triumph upon the face of Ohano?

Troubled, she begged her husband to tell her exactly of what they had talked in her absence. He reassured her, told her she but imagined a change; but he held her so closely, so savagely to his breast that she was surer than ever that something menaced their happiness.

The following morning she trembled and turned very pale at a sneering hint conveyed by the mother-in-law.

The fact that she was childless at the end of the first year, then, had become a subject of remark in the family!

The Lady Saito remarked sarcastically that among certain classes it was customary for childless women to drink of the Kiyomidzu Temple springs. They were said to contain miraculous qualities by which one might attain to motherhood.

Moonlight said nothing, but unconsciously her glance stole to her husband. He had grown uncomfortably red, and she saw his scowling face turned upon his mother.

Later, very timidly, she begged his permission to drink of the springs. He was opposed to it, saying it was a superstition of the ignorant; his mother but jested. She pleaded so insistently, and seemed to take the matter so deeply to heart, that at last he consented.

And so, with this last frantic hope, the geisha whose flashing beauty and talents had made her a queen in the most exacting of the tea-houses of Kioto now joined this melancholy band of childless women who thus desperately seek to please the gods by drinking of their favored waters.

XI

As a matter of expediency, the father told Gonji, it would be necessary to divorce Moonlight. One could not allow one's family to be wiped out because of a matter of mere sentiment and passion. Doubtless, the young wife, who had proved a most docile and obedient daughter-in-law in every way, would see the necessity of dissolving the union.

Gonji pleaded for time, one, two, three more years. Moonlight was very young. They could afford to wait.

His father, at heart as soft toward his son as his wife was stern, surrendered, as always.

"Arrange it with your mother, then. I am going to Tokio for a week."

It was a difficult subject to breach to his mother, and Gonji avoided it fearfully; nor did he mention the matter to his wife, whose wistful glance he had begun to avoid. Indeed, he saw less of his wife each day, for his mother was careful to keep the girl constantly employed in her service, and in the intervals of leisure Moonlight would go to the shrines or to the Kiyomidzu springs. Gonji, moreover, was making an effort to conceal somewhat of his affection for his wife from his mother in an effort to conciliate her; and he even made advances toward the older lady, waiting upon her with great thoughtfulness and seeming anxious for her constant comfort and happiness. But all his efforts met with satirical and acid remarks from his mother, and not for a moment did she change in her attitude to the young wife.

The subject, avoided as it had been by the young husband, was bound to come up at last. It was plain that it occupied the mind of Lady Saito at this time to the exclusion of all else. She broached it herself one morning at breakfast, when, besides her son and her daughter-in-law, Ohano was present, ostentatiously vying with the young wife in replenishing the older woman's plate and cup.

"Now," said Lady Saito, abruptly, turning over her rice bowl to signify her meal was ended, "it must be plain to both of you that things cannot continue as they are. The fate of all our ancestors is menaced. Come, Moonlight, lift up your head. Suggest some solution of the problem."

"I will double my offerings at the shrines," said the young creature, with quivering lips; and at the contemptuous movement of her mother-in-law, and the smile upon Ohano's face, she added, desperately: "I will wear my knees out, if necessary. I will not leave the springs at all, till the gods have heard my prayer."

Lady Saito tapped her finger irritably against the tobacco-bon. Ohano solicitously filled and lit the long-stemmed pipe, and refilled and relit it ere the mother of Gonji spoke again.

"Of course, it is very hard. So is everything in life—hard! We learn that as we grow older; but there are the comforting words of the philosophers. You should study well the 'Greater Learning for Women.' Really, my girl, you will find there is even a satisfaction in unselfishness."

Two red spots, hectic and feverish, stole into the waxen cheeks of the young wife. Her fingers writhed mechanically. Her eyes were riveted in fascination upon the face of the one who had tormented her now for so long. Wayward, passionate, savage impulses swept over her. She felt an intense longing to strike out—just once!

Something was touching her hand. Her fingers closed spasmodically about Gonji's. A sob rose stranglingly in her throat, but she held herself stiffly erect. Death, she felt, would be preferable, rather than that they should see how she was suffering.

The mother-in-law's voice droned on monotonously:

"I have been well advised in the matter. Yes, I even called in the counsel of your uncle, Ohano," turning toward Ohano, who was affectionately waiting upon her. "When your father returns, my children, there shall be a family council. Be assured, Moonlight, that, whatever comes, you will be properly supported by the Saito family for the rest of your days, though I have no doubt at all but that you will shortly marry. With a dowry from the Saito and a pretty face—well, a pretty face often accomplishes astonishing things. See the case of our own son. It was apparent to every one he was bewitched, obsessed! He would have his way! Contemplated suppuku! Forgot his duty to his parents, his ancestors—forgot that in Japan duty is higher than love. He made great promises. Well, we listened. At the time I bade him ponder the proverb: 'Beware of a beautiful woman. She is like red pepper!'—will burn, sting, is death to those who touch her, and—"

"Mother!"

"Is it a new custom to interrupt the head of the house?"

The young man's voice trembled with repressed feeling, but there was a certain expression of outraged dignity in his face as he looked at his mother fairly.

ONOTO WATANNA

"In the absence of the honorable father, the son is the legitimate head of the household," he said.

It was the first time he had spoken thus to her. He had restrained himself during this last year, for fear of bringing down his mother's wrath upon the defenseless head of Moonlight.

The hand that pounded the ash from her pipe trembled now, and her lips had become a thin, compressed line. She started to arise, but Ohano sprang to her assistance, and she leaned against the girl as she flung back, almost snarlingly, the words at her son:

"So be it, august authority! We will await the return of thy father. *He* will then decide the fate of this—"

"No, mother," he broke in, "I make humble apology. Speak your will, but pity us, your children. We desire to be filial, obedient, but it is cruel, hard!"

"Hard!" cried his mother, savagely. "Is it harder than for a mother to see her only son enmeshed in the web of a vile Spider?"

Moonlight had sprung up sharply now. Her eyes were like wells of fire as, her bosom heaving, she started toward the older woman. A grim smile distorted the features of the Lady Saito Ichigo. As the girl advanced toward her, with that unconsciously threatening motion, this old woman of patrician ancestry neither moved nor retreated a space. In her cold, sneering gaze one read the disdain of the woman of caste who sees one whom she deems beneath her betray her lowly origin.

"Moonlight!" She felt herself caught by the shoulders in a grip that almost pained. She caught but a glimpse of his face. It was livid. Feeling that he, too, was deserting her, she uttered a loud cry, and covering her face with her sleeve, she fled from the room.

And all that night she lay weeping and trembling in the arms of her husband. In vain he besought her not to abandon herself to such wild and terrible grief. Moonlight was very, very sure, she told him, that all the gods of the heavens and the seas had deserted her forever and forever. She dreamed of an abyss into which she was pushed and which closed inexorably about her, and from which not even the loving arms of the Lord Saito Gonji could rescue her.

XII

The quiet that comes before a tempest reigned for a few days in the household. Like a volcano whose pent-up energy is the more violent from long repression, it burst its bounds upon the return of the master.

Day and night they renewed the argument. Now Lord Ichigo was in firm agreement with his wife on the subject. There was no other course. Moonlight must go. Without descendants, who would there be to make the offerings and pray for their souls and those of the ancestors?

And again he was won over to his son's side. Well, it would do no harm to wait another year. Moonlight was, as they had pointed out, still very young and healthy. There was every likelihood that she would bear children.

Lady Saito, however, had set herself stubbornly against all truce. She was determined now to be rid of the Spider. The wretched geisha-girl, she alleged, had been forced into their illustrious family through the mere passion of a boy. It was a matter of humiliation that a child should have prevailed, in such a contention, over the parents. They should have vetoed the thing at the outset. Their love for their son should have but strengthened their resolve. The main thing now was to be rid of the incubus. The law was perfectly clear upon the matter. Never a simpler case. Doubtless, it was the workings of the gods, who pitied the ancestors. Here was a great family threatened with extinction. Should a thousand illustrious and heroic ancestors then be doomed to the cruelest of fates because of a notorious Spider woman? It were better, decreed the stern-minded lady, that the family commit honorable suppuku than suffer an extinction so contemptible.

Against such a flood of bitter argument and invective the young people could turn only their tears and their prayers.

Then it seemed as if the very hand of Fate intervened to settle the matter finally. The war with Russia had begun. The effect of this news upon the Saito family was electrical. It silenced the storm of cruel innuendo and abuse. It stopped the battle of words. All saw at once that the Lord Saito Gonji could now take but one course.

Following the steps of his ancestors, he must of course be in the foremost ranks of war. It would be his duty, his hope, to give up his life for the Mikado. Therefore, before leaving for the seat of war, it would be imperative that he should leave behind him in Japan a lineal descendant.

There was no need, the parents now felt assured, to speak another word of urging. Even the young wife, of lowly stock as she was, would see the necessity now of self-sacrifice.

Dry-eyed, pale, with leaden hearts, the young people now faced each other. The family had mercifully left them alone.

She sought to entrap his gaze, but persistently, gloomily, he averted his face. The delusion which had upheld her through all these dizzy, torturing months, that the gods had chosen one so humble as she to hand down the race of heroes, had dissolved now into thin air. Alas, how slender—ah, slenderer than the imaginary web she had spun as the Spider!—had been her hold upon the all-highest!

"Gonji! My Lord Gonji!" She caught at his hand, entreating his touch. "Do not turn your head. Speak to me. Pardon me that I have been unable to serve the ancestors—to please you, augustness!"

"You please me in all things," he said, roughly. "I *dare* not look at you—now!"

"It will give me strength if you will but condescend. The sacrifice will be sweet, if it gives your lordship pleasure!"

"Pleasure! Gods!"

He broke down completely and, like a child, buried his face upon her bosom. But no tears came to the relief of the girl. Tremulously, tenderly, she smoothed his hair.

Presently he put her from him and sat back looking at her now with hungry, somber eyes. She met his glance with a bright bravery. Their hands close-locked, they repeated solemnly together the promise to marry in all the lives yet to come and to travel the final journey to Nirvana together.

Then:

"There is satisfaction in performing a noble duty," said he, automatically.

And she:

"It is a privilege for one so humble to serve the exalted ancestors of your excellency in even so insignificant a way."

Silence a moment, during which he tried to speak, but could not. Then he burst out wildly:

"A thousand august ancestors call to me sternly from the noble past." He covered his eyes, lest the wistful, appealing beauty of her face might cause him to falter. "They entreat me not to extinguish their honorable spark of life. I am but the honorable custodian of the seed! I cannot prove recreant to its charge!"

A longer silence fell between them now, and when he dared again to look at her, he found she smiled, a gentle, brooding smile, such as a gentle mother might have turned upon him. It irradiated and made beautiful beyond words her thin little face.

"I will speak to my father!" he cried out, wildly. "It is not possible for me to put you away from me, beloved one!"

He made a savage movement toward her, as though again he would enfold her within his arms; but now, as he advanced, she retreated, her little speaking hands held before her, as though she pushed him from her.

"It is—as it should be! You are the all-highest one, and I—but a geisha. With this little hand I cannot dip up the ocean. I have tried, august one, and—and—its waters have engulfed me!"

"I go to service of Tenshi-sama!" he cried, hoarsely. "We may never meet again in this honorable life, but, ah, there are a thousand lives we can be sure to share together!"

"A—thousand—lives—together!" she repeated, her eyes closed, her face as white as one dead.

Slowly, feeling backward with her hands, she groped her way to the shoji. There she paused a moment and looked at her husband, a long, deep, enveloping look.

He heard the sliding doors trapped between them, and listened vainly for even the softest fall of her footsteps. But the geisha moves with the silence of a moth, and the one who had gone from him forever, as it seemed, had broken her wings against his heart.

XIII

So the Lord Saito Gonji went to Tokio the following day, and immediately the machinery of law, which grinds less slowly in Japan than in many other countries, was set in motion. All that wealth, power, influence could do to hasten matters was brought to bear. Presently the wife of Lord Gonji was divorced by her husband's parents and legally barred from the home of his ancestors.

No one knew where she had gone. Disregarding and refusing all the charitable and gracious offers and promises of present or future aid, she disappeared upon the night of her last interview with her husband, going without even the customary ceremonious leave-taking.

Even her going, pointed out the relatives, was proof of her unworthiness. The daughter of a samourai would have departed with a certain submissive dignity and grace, and, whatever her lacerated feelings, would have proclaimed her pleasure in the act of the superior ones. But the geisha-girl fled in the night, like one who goes in fear and shame.

Meanwhile Ohano was duly taken to Tokio. Here in the presence of a host of triumphantly joyous and exultant relatives she was married at last to the Lord Saito Gonji.

Here, like a dutiful wife, she remained in the capital by her husband's side, awaiting the summons which would take him from her and give him eternally to the Emperor.

As a little boy Gonji had been, in a way, fond of Ohano. She was of that chubby, sulky type that a small boy delights to tease. Time had changed very little the form and disposition of Ohano; but what in a child had appealed to his humorous affection, in a woman proved not merely tiresome but repellent. Mere unadorned flesh has little attraction for one of a naturally poetic and visionary temperament. Even the slight affection he had felt for Ohano as a child had now entirely disappeared. It was with an element of positive loathing that he regarded the girl he had married. When his mind reverted to the one he had forsaken on her account, he was filled with such overwhelming despair that it seemed as if he must injure himself—but for the mighty events in which he tried vainly to plunge his mind.

No soldier in all the Emperor's service, though animated with the most lofty patriotism and excitement as the times demanded, seized upon the cause with such fanatic zeal as Lord Gonji. Day and night he was among his men. When not in some way improving their equipment and physical condition, he was arousing and stimulating their ardor and patriotism.

People pointed with pride to the young man's heroic ancestry, and prophesied that in his young body still glowed that wonderful spark which would give to Japan another hero, and assure for all under him glorious victory and triumph.

It seemed as if it were impossible for him to leave his men even to return to his temporary home for rest and sleep. The prayers and entreaties of his mother and of his new wife fell upon deaf ears. Vainly they besought him, in the short time he was yet to be in Japan, to remain as much as possible in their company. They were sacrificing him for all time. Surely even exalted Tenshi-sama (the Mikado) would not begrudge to them the little, precious moments he might yet spend in Japan.

Gonji looked at the pleading women with blank, cold eyes. Then, abruptly, he would return to his labors.

Never since the day they had married him to Ohano had he voluntarily addressed a single word to his wife. When forced finally at night to return to her sole company, he would creep back stealthily to the house like some guilty wretch entering upon some infamous errand. There, always, he found her patiently, dutifully awaiting his coming.

"My dear lord," she would humbly say, "though it is very late, I pray you feed the honorable insides. Permit the honorable interior to wait upon your excellency."

He ignored the tray of viands thus nightly tendered him as completely as he did her words; but when she made officious efforts to assist him to undress, kneeling in the attitude of a servant or the lowliest of wives, to wash his feet, he would quietly push her to one side, just as though she were some article that stood in his pathway.

Sometimes he would point silently to his wife's couch, thus sternly bidding her retire. When this was accomplished, he would lie down beside her, and not till the heavy, even, healthy breathing of Ohano proclaimed she slept would he close his own weary eyelids.

Beside Ohano's blooming, satisfied face (for with feminine logic Ohano set her husband's curious treatment of her down to his absorption in the war matter, and thus in the proud knowledge of possession still found happiness), he conjured up always that thin, white, wistful one, whose long dark eyes had drawn the very heart out of his breast from the moment they had first looked into his own.

Sometimes in the night he would arise, to tramp frenziedly up and down, as he pictured the fate that might have befallen the beloved Moonlight. What had become of her? Whither had she gone? How would she fare, now that, penniless and without even her old employment (for now in time of war the geishas were in reduced circumstances), she had been cast adrift?

He cursed his own folly in not having foreseen the way in which she would go; for not having provided for her, forced her to accept at least monetary assistance of some kind from his family.

His agents had assured him she had not returned to Matsuda; neither had a trace been found of her in any of the geisha-houses of Tokio or Kioto. Whither, then, had she gone? A sick fear seized upon him that she had started upon the Long Journey alone, without waiting for him, who had promised to tread it with her. He knew that he would never know a moment's peace till the time when, face to face, they should meet each other upon the Long Road which has no ending.

Thus the wretched nights passed, giving the unhappy man little or no rest; and that he might not encounter the ingratiating smiles and questions of Ohano, he would depart hurriedly ere she awoke, and plunge into the war preparations with renewed fervor and desperation.

XIV

The days stretched into weeks; the weeks into months. It is not possible to account for the various delays that arise in time of war. Four months had passed since his marriage to Ohano, when at last the welcome summons came. His honorable regiment was to go to the front!

Gonji felt like one released from a cruel bondage. His very heart leaped within him like a mad thing. Even to Ohano he spoke, and although his words had a deep ulterior meaning, she was gratified and elated. They stood as a proof at least to her of her elevation. He had noticed her! Undoubtedly she had leaped forward a thousand paces in the estimation of her lord. He recognized her importance now at the crucial moment.

Naturally vain and proud, Ohano's mind had been entirely concerned with the attention she was attracting from all as the wife of the Lord Saito Gonji. People pointed her out as she rode abroad in the lacquered carriages of the Saito family, and everywhere was recounted the illustrious history of his ancestors and of her own important mission, now when the last of the exalted race was sacrificing his life for Japan.

And now her lord himself had condescended to notice her, and for the first time his somewhat wild eyes had looked at Ohano with an element of gentleness and kindness. His words were curious, and long after he was gone to the city Ohano turned them over in her mind and pondered their meaning; and when, that night, he returned to her for the last time, she begged him to repeat them, saying that the presence of the parents-in-law had confused her hearing. She wished rightly and clearly to understand his words, so that when he was quite gone from her she might the better carry out his wishes.

With solemn dignity he repeated the instructions:

"Take care of your honorable health and of that of my descendant. Choose wisely a companion upon the Long Journey, for it is lonely to travel. The world is peopled with many souls, but only two may travel the final path together."

Again she pondered the words, and she shivered under her husband's melancholy glance. What did the strange words imply? Consideration for her future merely? Surely he must know that, as the wife of one so illustrious as he must become, she would never marry another in his place. (Every Japanese woman resigns her husband to war service with the proud and pious belief and hope that he will not return, but will gloriously sacrifice life for the cause.)

Finally she said, as she watched his face stealthily:

"It will be unnecessary for the humble one to choose another companion. Glorious will be the privilege of awaiting the time when she will join your honor on the journey."

He gave her a deep look, which seemed to pierce and search to the very depths of her heart.

"Ohano," he said, "*thou* knowest I did not marry thee save for the time of this life."

She sat up stiffly, mechanically, moistening her dry lips. All the petty vanity with which she had upheld herself since the day when she had married Saito Gonji now seemed to drop from her in shreds. Her many days of supreme devotion, and even adoration, for the Lord Gonji—and they stretched back as far as her childhood days—came up to torture her. Looking into her husband's face, Ohano knew, without questioning, who it was who would make the final precious journey with him. She was to be wife only for the short span of his lifetime. That other one, the Spider—whose image in effigy she had pricked so mercilessly with a thousand spiteful pins in order to destroy her soul, as she fain would have done her body—*she* was to be the wife of Saito Gonji for all time! She who had stolen him from Ohano upon her very wedding-night!

Her face became convulsed. The eyes seemed to have disappeared from her face. Presently, breathing heavily, her hands clutching her breast to repress the emotion which would show despite her best efforts:

"I pray you permit your humble wife to attend your lordship upon the journey," she said. "Who else is competent to travel at your side, my lord?"

He did not answer her. He was looking out of an open shoji, and his face in the moonlight seemed as if carved in marble, so set, so rigid, immovable as that of one dead.

Ohano rose desperately to her feet. She felt unspeakably weak from the excess of her inner passion. At that moment gladly would she have exchanged places with the homeless and outcast wife of Saito Gonji, who in the end was to come to that eternal bliss so rigorously denied to Ohano.

She caught at her husband's hand. He drew it up into his sleeve. There had never been any caresses between them. Always he seemed rather to shrink from contact with her.

"Lord, let us call a family council," she cried, shrilly. "Let them decide where is my proper place, Lord Saito Gonji. It is not for the time of one life only that we marry. I have plighted my troth to you for all time!"

Slowly he turned; and the deep, penetrating look scorched Ohano again.

"And I," he said, "have plighted my troth with another."

"Lord, it was dissolved," she cried, breathlessly, "by the honorable laws of our land. The Spider is now an outcast. Ah!"—her voice rose shrilly on the verge of hysteria—"it is said—it is known—proved by those who know—that now—now she is an inmate of the Yoshiwara. She—"

He had gripped her so savagely by the shoulder that she cried aloud in pain. At her cry he threw her from him almost as if she had been some unclean thing. She fell upon her knees, and upon them crept toward him, stretching out her hands and beating them futilely together.

"My Lord Gonji! My husband! I am your honorable wife before all the eight million gods of the heavens and the seas. It is impossible to forsake me. I will not permit it. I will cling to your skirts and proclaim my rights—ah, yes, to the very doors of Hades, if need be!"

He seemed not even to hear her. With his face thrust out like one who dreams, he was recalling a vision. It was the face of Moonlight as he had seen it last with that exalted, spiritual expression of self-sacrifice and adoration upon it. *She* an inmate of the cursed Yoshiwara! The thought was grotesque, so horrible that a short laugh came to his lips.

He strode by the agonized woman on the floor without a further word, and sharply snapped the folding doors between them. This was their farewell.

As he passed down the street, on his way to join his regiment, he was halted by the throngs pressing on all sides. The whole country seemed to be abroad in the streets. The people marched about carrying banners, and even the little children seemed to have caught the spirit of Yamato Damashii (the Soul of Japan), and stammered their little banzais in chorus. It was an inspiring sight, and he wandered about for some time, with no particular purpose, unconscious where he was, in what direction his feet carried him, following the throngs as they pushed along through the streets.

Suddenly he came to where the lights were brighter; and the sounds of revelry seemed to shriek at the very gates. Gonji paused, concentrating his attention for the first time upon the place.

All at once it dawned upon him that he was before the gates of the Yoshiwara! The words of Ohano seemed to ring in his ears. As if to shut out their loud outcry, he covered his ears and sped like a madman down the street. He swore to his very soul that it was an accursed lie Ohano had uttered, and yet—

He stopped suddenly and threw a furtive, agonized glance toward the infernal "city." Then his head drooped down upon his breast and he staggered toward the barracks like one who has been wounded mortally.

XV

Let us go outside. See, many of the citizens stand on the roofs of the cars. We can see nothing from here."

Thus coaxed Ohano. With Gonji's parents she was traveling, their train running parallel with another crowded with the departing troops. The trains moved slowly, for all the country had come to see the departing ones and to acclaim them with loud banzais.

Lady Saito's hard features were unrecognizable because of their swollen and agonized appearance. She allowed the younger woman to support her and finally draw her outside. The people made way respectfully for them. Every one knew their history—knew, moreover, of the sacrifice they were making in giving up the only son, and of how generously they had contributed to the war fund. Here were the brave, patriotic father and mother! Here the young and beautiful wife.

Ohano's round cheeks were pink with excitement. She had forgotten, for the time being at least, her last interview with her husband. The excitement of the situation, the murmured admiration and respect of those about her, upheld her. There was almost an element of enjoyment mingled with her excitement, as her eyes wandered eagerly over the crowds.

The train bearing the troops moved a bit swifter along its course, and the fourth car came opposite to that on the platform of which stood the Saito family.

"There he is! There he is!" cried Ohano, excitedly; and she leaned far out, restrained by the solicitous hand of her father-in-law, and, waving her silk handkerchief, called to her husband by name:

"Gonji! Gonji! My Lord Gonji!"

"My son!" moaned the aged woman, unable longer to restrain her feelings.

Stoically, and with no sign of the ache within her, she had parted from her son. Japanese women send their men on perilous journeys with smiles upon their lips, even while their hearts are breaking; but now, as the mother saw the train carrying away the only child the gods had given her, the tension broke. She clung moaning to her husband and her daughter-in-law.

For the first time, as she saw the thin profile of the young man in the window of the car opposite, she was seized with an overwhelming sense of remorse. What happiness had she ever helped to bring into the life of her boy? She had put him from her after the manner of a Spartan woman while he was yet in tender years. She had done this fiercely, heroically as she believed, fearing that otherwise she might not sufficiently do her duty to both him and the ancestors. But now—now! He was going from her forever! She had given him to the Emperor! Soon her terrible prayer that he might give his young life in service for his Emperor and country might indeed be answered.

She felt very old, very feeble, and utterly forsaken and forlorn. Even as she looked through tear-blinded eyes at her son there came vividly before her memory the pale and tragic face of the young and outcast wife he had loved so passionately. She burst into a loud cry, stretching out her arms frantically:

"Oh, my son! Oh, my son!"

In the opposite train Gonji raised his head, saw his people, but, possibly because of the crowds and the intervening glass pane, did not notice their intense anguish. He smiled, bowed, and made a slight motion of salute with his hand.

His mother was silenced, and remained staring at him like one turned to stone. Ohano's face fell, and she stood like a pouting child unjustly punished. He had not even risen in his seat nor so much as opened the window.

Both trains had now come to a standstill at the little suburban station. Crowds of people swarmed over the platform, some even climbing the steps of the troop-train and penetrating into the cars themselves. A band began to beat out the monotonous droning music of the national hymn. Windows were raised, caps lifted, and cheering ensued for a time. But still the Lord Gonji remained unmoved, not rousing from the moody reverie into which he seemed plunged, and casting not even a glance in the direction of the party that watched him so eagerly from across the way: so oblivious and indifferent to his surroundings did he seem.

Suddenly an officer in the seat behind him leaned over and spoke to him. His family saw Gonji start as if he had been struck. Turning about quickly in his seat, he tore at the fastenings of the window. Now he leaned far out, his ears strained, his eyes searching above the vast crowds without.

They watched him curiously, following his gaze. His lips moved; he seemed about to leap from the window, but was held back by the restraining hand of his brother-officer, and the train began to move rapidly.

A hush had fallen not alone upon the family of the Saito, but on the throngs pressing on all sides. As if compelled, their united gaze followed that of the seemingly entranced Gonji.

Upon a little hillock a short space removed from the station, one lone figure stood out, silhouetted against the clear blue sky. Her kimono was of a vermilion color, embroidered with dragons of gold. Gold, too, was her obi, and in the bright sunlight her scarlet fan and the poppies in her hair flashed like sparks of fire.

To the crowds in the valley below, surging like a swarm of sheep all along the railway-tracks, following the troop-trains, their hoarse cheers mingling with that of the beating drums and the chanting of the national hymn, she seemed a symbol of triumph, an exquisite omen of victory to come!

Some one shouted her name aloud:

"The glorious Spider of the House of Slender Pines!"

"Nay," cried another, "it is the vision of the Sun Lady herself!"

The soldiers, too, saw her, and began to cheer, their wild banzais ringing out triumphantly and reaching the geisha on the hill.

XVI

On a day in the season of greatest heat, a few months after the going of Lord Saito Gonji to the front, there staggered up the tortuous and winding pathway, which climbed the mountain-side to where the House of Slender Pines rested as on a cliff, a curious figure. She was garbed in the conventional dress of the geisha, and the burning sun, beating down upon the little figure, showed the gold of her wide obi and the glittering vermilion of her kimono.

Something bound to the woman's neck and back seemed to crush her almost double beneath its weight, and she clung weakly to the stumps of tree and bush as she made her way along.

It seemed almost, to the geishas sitting in the cool shade of the pavilion, that she dragged herself along on her hands and knees.

One ceased strumming upon the samisen, and a dancer, idly illustrating a few new gestures to the admiring apprentices, stopped in the middle of a movement.

Omi suddenly screeched and caught at the sleeve of the dancer. No one moved or spoke. They stood dumbfounded, staring with unbelieving eyes at the Spider, as she crept up the last height and dropped in silent exhaustion in their midst. There, with the glowing sun beating mercilessly down upon her, entangled in her glimmering gown, she lay like a great dead butterfly.

There was a stir among the geishas. Eyes met eyes in meaning, shocked glances; but still, from custom, they were voiceless.

Suddenly the little Omi began to run about like one bereft of her senses. One moment she knelt by her former mistress; the next she sought to awaken the chaperon, shaking and pounding that enormously stout and somnolent lady. Several maids now joined her, and they ran about in panic-stricken circles, uncertain what to do. Matsuda was absent. The poor, mindless Okusama was indoors, playing and talking with her countless dolls, quite oblivious of all about her. Should they go to her? Would she understand?

Omi finally darted into the house, and, dragging the Okusama from her dolls, drew her out into the sunlight. For a moment the demented creature stared with a puzzled, troubled look at the form upon the ground. Then she began to utter strange little inarticulate cries and threw herself upon the body of the Spider.

She seemed suddenly to regain all of her lost senses. She felt the geisha's hands, listened to her heart, screamed for water, and tore at the object upon the Spider's back, drawing it warmly to her own bosom.

One maiden brought water, another a parasol, another a fan, while Omi supported Moonlight's head upon her lap. One vied with the other in performing some service for the one they all had loved.

Presently the heavy eyes of the Spider opened, and, dazedly, she appeared to recognize the faces of those about her. A faint smile crept to her white lips. But the smile quickly faded, and a piteous look of commingled fear and pain stole over her wan little face. She put back her hands to her neck and started up, moaning. Loving arms were about her. They reassured her that all about her were friends, and showed her her baby, where, safe and sweet, it rested in the bosom of the Okusama. Then for a long time she lay with her eyes closed, a look of peace, such as comes after a long, exhausting race, upon her face.

Later, when, refreshed and stronger, she rested among the geishas in the pavilion, she weakly and somewhat incoherently told them the story of her wanderings.

At first she had found employment under another name in a tea-house of the city of Tokio; but it was not in the capacity of geisha, for she knew the agents of her husband sought among all the houses of the two cities for a geisha answering her description. Moreover, she had not the heart nor the strength to follow her old employment. So she had worked in the humble capacity of seamstress to a geisha-house in Tokio, near by the very barracks where her husband daily went. Every day she had seen him, unseen by him. She had even heard his inquiries of the master of the house for one answering her description. But no one had thought of the pale and shrinking little sewing woman, who so humbly served the geishas, as the famous one they sought.

Then the war had caused business stagnation everywhere in Tokio, and the first to suffer were the geishas. Patrons now were few, confined mostly to members of the departing regiments.

Moonlight's strength at this time had begun to fail her. Her work was unsatisfactory. She was dismissed. Now, at this time, when it was too late to please the Lord Saito Gonji and all his august ancestors, she had made the astonishing discovery, which she had not known when with him: that she was to become a mother!

Unable, even had she so desired, to return to the house of the Saitos, scorning to accept even the smallest help from the family which had divorced her, turned away from every place where she sought employment because of her condition, she had been reduced to the direst necessity. Indeed she, the once celebrated Spider, the wife of the noble Lord Saito Gonji, had become a miserable mendicant, hovering on the outskirts of the temples and the tea-houses, seeking, in the garb of her late calling, now worn and tattered, as they saw, for pity and charity. After long and tortuous wanderings, she had at last managed to return to Kioto. She wandered out into the hills in search of the House of Slender Pines.

In a secluded and quiet little corner of a seemingly deserted and unexplored hill she had found at last a refuge in a diminutive temple, where a lonely priestess expiated the sins of her youth by a life of absolute solitude and piety. Here Moonlight's child was born. Here she might still have been, but the aged nun had finished her last penance and had gone to join the ones the gods loved in Nirvana. The geisha had set out again, in search of her former home, and now she bore her baby on her back. Without funds to pay for a jinrikisha, she had traveled entirely on foot. The journey had been long, the sun never so hot, but, ah! the gods had guided her feet unerringly, and here at last she was in their midst!

She looked at the Okusama, whispering to the little head against her lips; at Omi, holding her hands in a strangling grasp and making violent contortions of her face in an effort to keep back the tears; at the geishas and maidens, with their pretty faces running over with tears. Then she sighed and smiled.

The Okusama seemed to remember something of a sudden. She started upon her knees, clapping her hands violently.

"Hurry, maidens!" she cried, shrilly. "The most honorable Spider requires new apparel! Wait upon her quickly and excellently!"

Omi whirled around in a dizzy circle, and she danced every step of the way to the house. Inside they heard her singing, and a moment later berating and scolding the maid who was to wait upon her mistress.

XVII

Returning from a fruitless canvass for patrons for his house, Matsuda was in an evil mood. The times were bitter. Upon every tongue was heard but the one topic—the war! The gayest and most spendthrift of youths turned a deaf ear to the geisha-keeper's descriptions of the exceptional beauty and talents of his maidens. The clash of drum and arms had a more alluring call to the men of Japan than the most charming song ever sung by geisha; and the glittering sun-flag, tossing aloft from every roof and tower, was more enchanting to their sight than the brightest pair of eyes or reddest lips of which the master of the geishas told.

Not a patron in all the city of Kioto for the once famous House of Slender Pines! Superstitiously its master feared his place was doomed.

At the solicitation of his wife, he had kept the girls despite the hard times; now he felt he could no longer humor even the Okusama. Matsuda knew the fate likely to befall the geishas, were they to be turned out of employment at this time. Unable to obtain positions through the customary channels of the geisha-houses, they had but one last resource—the Yoshiwara! Even in war-times the "hell city," as it was aptly named, thrived. Against this fate the Okusama had so far shielded the geishas of the House of Slender Pines, and even now, as he thought of her, Matsuda debated how he should explain the going of even the humblest apprentice.

As his jinrikisha wound in and out up the twisting pathway, he noted through the shadowing trees that the tea-house was brilliantly lighted, an expense lately considerably cut down by his express orders. The frown upon his brow grew darker, and his little cruel eyes were like those of a wild boar.

As he turned into the gates he saw that even the pathway was strung with lighted lanterns, and from the house itself came the resounding beat of the triumphant little koto, mingled with the softly humming voices of the geishas.

The illuminated tea-house, the music, the air of festivity and affluence puzzled him. It was against his orders, but, perchance, in his absence, some lofty ones had condescended to patronize his place!

As he stepped from his carriage, the laughing little Omi came running down to the gate to meet him, a bowl of water splashing in her hands. So eager she seemed to welcome the master, she barely waited for him to kick aside his clogs ere she dashed the refreshing water upon his heated feet.

The geishas prostrated themselves as he passed among them. Wherever he looked he saw the lights and the evidences of a recent feast; but nowhere did the master of the geishas see a single guest.

His face had become pastily white, and his little eyes glittered as they turned from side to side. So far he spoke no word to the offending geishas. Looking upward, he noted the illuminated second story, while the lighted takahiras were visible against the massed flowers of the balconies and the tingling wind-bells. But still, nowhere a guest! Mystified, his rage deepening, he turned suddenly with a roar toward the geishas.

So this was the way his servants disported themselves in his absence! Feasting and celebrating! So be it. They were shortly to learn that their master carried with him a punishment even more dreadful than the whip. "The Yoshiwara!" he shouted, raising his clenched fists above his head. That was the fate reserved for the faithless cattle he had trusted.

No one stirred. No one spoke. The geishas, still prostrated, kept their humble heads on the ground. Yet something in their unshrinking attitude made him see that for some reason they did not realize his words. Like an animal in pain, he bounced into their midst, his arm upraised to strike, his foot to kick.

Some one caught at his sleeve and held to it insistently. He turned and encountered the white, wild face of his wife. Her lips moved voicelessly, but she clung with tenacity to his sleeve.

For the first time he struck the Okusama—a cruel, savage blow that sent her staggering back from him. She sprang back to his side, dumbly caught again at his sleeve with one hand, and pointed steadily upward with the other.

Matsuda looked and began to shake. There on the widest balcony of the House of Slender Pines, swaying and tossing like a moth in the wind, the Spider spun her web.

He wiped his eyes as if to make sure he did not see a vision; but still the alluring, smiling face of the one who had brought him fortune glanced at him in the torchlight.

"The Spider!" he cried hoarsely. "She is back!"

XVIII

O f course, figured Matsuda to himself, even the addition of one so famous as the Spider could not at once bring fortune to the House of Slender Pines at war-time. Then, too, there was the honorable child to sustain.

Not for a moment, Matsuda told himself, did he begrudge or regret the celebrations in the Spider's honor rightly insisted upon by his wife. Undoubtedly she was an honorable guest. Still, a poor man, the keeper of a half-score of geishas, must make proper provision for their future sustenance and his own old age. If the Spider were, in fact, to prove her old title of fortune-bringer to the geisha-house, it was necessary that she begin at once.

So, while the Okusama and the geishas showered the Spider with favors and waited upon her slightest wish, while the honorable descendant of the illustrious Saito blood joyously passed from hand to hand, while the Okusama cast aside her dolls and hovered like a brooding mother over Moonlight and her baby, Matsuda held his head within his own chamber and cunningly planned a scheme whereby the Spider's presence in his house might be turned to immediate profit.

By his contract with the Saito family, the Spider was released from bondage. Hence she was not entirely bound to serve him. She had already excited his exasperation by her persistent refusal to dance for prospective customers the dance by which she had won fame. She desired to assume another pseudonym, and for a month at least asked that she might rest and thus regain her strength.

A month! inwardly had snorted Matsuda. Why, even the last batch of troops would be at the front by then. Japan would be emptied completely of her men. Now was the time, if ever, to draw patrons to the house, since the departing soldiers celebrated their going at the most popular geisha-houses. Only the fact that the House of Slender Pines was some distance away among the hills kept the soldiers from patronizing it in preference to those in the city of Kioto. But, could Matsuda venture down below, proclaiming the fact of the return of the Spider, ah, then indeed he might be assured of customers for a time at least!

No amount of pleading or reasoning, however, moved the Spider. With the pitying, solicitous, fond arms of the Okusama about her, she languidly proclaimed herself still ill, as indeed she looked and was.

So Matsuda chewed on his nails and thought and thought. He thought of the agents of the young Lord Saito Gonji, who had come to see him at the time Gonji's regiment was stationed in Tokio. He thought of the exorbitant reward temptingly tendered him for any information of the Spider. How he had cursed his inability to find the girl at that time. But the young Lord Gonji was gone—gone forever, undoubtedly. Who was there in all this haughty family, which had disdainfully and contemptuously cast out from its doors the miserable geisha, who could now possibly be interested in her lot? Nevertheless, the master of the geisha-house pondered the matter, and as he did so there came up suddenly before his mind's eye the round rosy face of the rightful heir of all the Saito ancestors. His heart began to thump within him with a strange excitement. Suddenly he set out upon a journey.

XIX

The ancestral home of the Saitos was situated in the most aristocratic of the suburbs of Kioto. Walled in on all sides by the evergreen hills and mountains and sharing in eminence and beauty the most famous of the temples, the shiro should have proved an ideal retreat for the saddened female relatives of the Lord Saito Gonji.

Here, with their household reduced to a single man and maid, and themselves performing menial tasks the more to chasten their spirits, as had become the custom during this period among the nobility, the mother and the wife of Saito Gonji lived silently together. For even the father of Gonji had heard the stern voice of Hachiman, the god of war, and had taken up arms dutifully in his Emperor's defense.

No longer was the harsh, sarcastic tongue of the Lady Saito Ichigo heard in insistent berating of maid and daughter-in-law; nor did the loud, mirthless laughter of Ohano ring out. Mute, their white faces marked with the shadow of a fear that fairly ate at their hearts' core, the two Saito women plodded along daily together.

For a time, after the going of Gonji, the older woman had waited upon the younger; but as the days and weeks passed her solicitude for the health of the young wife slowly diminished, and in its place came a scorching anxiety to torture the now aging woman.

Not in the sneering tone she had turned upon the hapless Moonlight, but with the deepest earnestness, she now besought her daughter-in-law daily to lavish costly offerings at the shrines, and even to drink of the Kiyomidzu springs! As became a dutiful daughter, the once smiling, taunting Ohano joined that same melancholy group where once the unhappy Moonlight had been a familiar figure.

Thus the tragic months passed away. Few if any words now passed between the Saito women. A wall seemed to have arisen between them. Where previously the older woman had felt for Ohano an affection almost equivalent to that of a mother, she now turned wearily from the girl's timid effort to appease her. Unlike, however, her treatment of the Spider, she at least spared the young wife the harsh, nagging, condemnatory words of reproach and recrimination.

Every morning the selfsame question was asked and answered:

"You were at Kiyomidzu yesterday, my daughter?"

"Hé, honorable mother."

"And—?"

"The gods are obdurate, alas!"

Lady Saito would mechanically knock out the ash from her pipe and refill it with her trembling fingers. Then, shaking her head, she would mutter:

"From the decree of heaven there is no escape!"

XX

E ven a calamity, left alone, may turn into a fortune," quoted Lady Saito Ichigo, devoutly, as with her hand trembling with excitement she filled her pipe.

Ohano listlessly extended the taper to her mother-in-law, and the latter took several puffs and inhaled with intense satisfaction.

There was something peculiarly still and strange about the attitude of Ohano. Her eyes seemed almost closed, her lips were a single colorless line, and there was not a vestige of color in her face. Almost she seemed like some automaton that was unable to move save when touched. One of Ohano's arms was shorter than the other, and this had always been a sensitive matter to her, so that generally she had carried it hidden in her sleeve. Now she nursed it mechanically, almost as if it pained, and twice she extended the lame arm for the taper. Whatever there was about the girl's expression or attitude, it aroused the irritation of the older woman, and she said sharply:

"You perceive the wisdom of the proverb, my girl, do you not?"

Ohano said slowly, as though the words came from her with an effort:

"It is not apropos to our case at all. I do not at all see either the calamity or the fortune, for that matter."

Her mother-in-law took her pipe from her mouth and stared at her amazedly a moment. Then she enumerated events upon her fingers.

"Calamity," she said, "when my son met the Spider woman. Almost it seemed as if the gods had forsaken their favorites. What a fate for the illustrious ancestors—the last of the race married to a geisha!"

Ohano shrugged her shoulders, then averted her face. She had bitten her lips so that now they seemed to be blistered, and pushed out, thick and swollen.

"Well," resumed her mother, triumphantly, "you perceive the workings of the gods undoubtedly in what followed. The war came like a veritable miracle. Think; had it come but a few—one or two—months later even, the Spider would still have been in our house, and, what is more, Ohano, elevated! Oh, there would have been no enduring the dancer. It is said"—and she lowered her voice confidently—"that the arrogance and pride of women of her class is an intolerable thing when once aroused. An excellent actress was this Spider. Let us admit it. She was prepared to—

wait! She entreated patience for only a few months longer. But, as I have said, the gods intervened. The war arose! It was found imperative to return her at once! Hoom! That is right. You may well smile, my girl, since your turn had come!"

Ohano's mask-like countenance had broken into a rigid smile of reminiscence. She recalled the days of her supreme triumph—the casting out of the one she hated, her own elevation as the wife of the Lord Saito Gonji. A faint color stole into her cheeks.

"I'll confess," continued the mother-in-law, humorously, "that you proved a less docile and filial daughter." She chuckled reminiscently. "It is impossible to forget the humility of the Spider!" She looked at Ohano fondly. "I will tell you, my girl, I always desired you for my daughter. Your mother and I were cousins, and do you know—I will tell you, now that my lord is honorably absent—that it was originally planned that your father and I should marry." She scowled and blinked her eyes, sighing heavily. "Well, schemes fall through!"

For a time she was silent, drowsily pulling at her pipe, which Ohano mechanically filled and refilled.

Presently Lady Saito laid her pipe down on the hibachi and resumed as if she had not stopped.

"So much for the calamity—the intervention of the gods that followed. Now look you, my girl. All the expensive offerings heaped at the shrines have been in vain. It is my opinion that if you supplicated the gods till doomsday and drank of the last drop of the Kiyomidzu waters, you would not now become a mother! Superstitions are for the ignorant. These are enlightened days, when we fight and beat—and *beat*, Ohano!—the Western nations! So, now, we supplicate the gods for a solution of the tragic problem facing us—the extinction of the illustrious race of Saito. It is impossible for such a race to die!"

Ohano moved uneasily. She had picked up her embroidery frame, and was attempting to work, but her lips were moving and her hands trembled. Partly to hide her expression from her mother-in-law, she bent her head far over the frame. Lady Saito began to laugh quite loudly.

"Never—no, not within the entire span of a lifetime—have I even heard of such favor of the gods! Just think, Ohano, without the pains and labors of a mother, they put into your honorable arms a most noble descendant of the august ancestors. Why, you should extend your arms in perpetual thanks to all the gods. Was ever such mercy?"

Said Ohano, with her face still hidden by the frame:

"It is said, as you know, that it is easier to beget children than to care for them!"

Silence a moment. Then she added with sudden passionate vehemence:

"I loathe the task you set me, mother-in-law. It is not possible for me to carry out your wishes."

The expression on the older woman's face should have warned her. The thin lips drew back in a line as cruel as when previously she had looked at the hapless Moonlight. Her voice was, if possible, harsher.

"It is better to nourish a dog than an unfaithful child!" she cried, got to her feet, and, drawing her skirts about her, moved away in stately dudgeon.

Ohano leaped up also, anxious to repair the injury she had done.

"Mother!" she cried out, chokingly, "put yourself in my place. Would it be possible for you to cherish in your bosom the child of one you abhorred?"

Slowly the outraged and angry look faded from Lady Saito's face. It seemed pinched and haggard. Her voice was curiously gentle:

"That is possible, Ohano. I have given you an instance in my own honorable house, for as deeply as I hated your mother, so I have loved you!"

Ohano's breath came in gasps. She was losing control of the icy nerve that had hitherto upheld her. She longed to fling herself upon the breast of her mother-in-law, who, despite her austere bearing to all, had always been kind to Ohano. Even as the two looked into each other's face the cry of the one they were expecting to arrive was heard outside the screens. Matsuda had kept his word!

Ohano turned white with despair. She clutched at her throat as though she were choking and clung for a moment to the screens, her anguished face turned back toward her mother-in-law.

"It is a crime!" she gasped. "The Spider will come for her child!"

"Let her come," darkly rejoined Lady Saito. "Who will take the word of a public geisha against that of the honorable ladies of the house of Saito?"

"The man—he himself—will betray—it is not possible to close the tongue of one of the choum class."

"He is well paid. Moreover, in committing the act he places himself under the ban of the law. Will he betray himself?"

Lady Saito moved with a curious sense of hunger toward the doors, outside which, she knew, was the son of her son. For the moment at least she had forgotten Ohano; but when she found the girl barred her passage she thrust her ruthlessly aside. Ohano fell upon her knees by the shoji, and, with her face hidden upon the floor, she began to pray to the gods.

XXI

Meanwhile in the House of Slender Pines there was pandemonium. The frightened, panic-stricken geishas and maidens fled wildly about, seeking in every nook and corner of the place for the lost child, while above their chattering and awe-stricken whispers rose the shrill, hysterical laughter of the Okusama.

She it was who had lost the child, so she averred, for it was upon her bosom the little one had slept.

Of all the inmates of the House of Slender Pines, the only one whose voice had not yet been heard was the geisha Moonlight. She sat in an upper chamber, her chin pillowed by her folded hands, while her long, dark eyes stared straight out before her blankly. She had remained in this motionless position from the moment they had told her of the loss of her child. Her little apprentice, Omi, fearing that her mistress's mind was affected, hung about her in tears, alternately offering bodily service and seeking to tempt the silent one to eat. But her offices were ignored or passively endured. The food remained untouched.

Not even the wild crying of the Okusama stirred her, though she could plainly hear the coaxing voices of the maidens as they sought to restrain her from flinging herself down the mountain-side.

Later in the day, however, when the Okusama, whose wailing, from sheer exhaustion, had turned to long gasping sobs, scratched and pulled at the shoji of the Spider's room, Moonlight stirred, like one coming out of a trance, and drew her hand dazedly across her eyes as she listened to the heartrending words of the Okusama.

"Dearest Moonlight! The honorable little one has gone upon a journey. He was too beautiful, too exalted for a geisha-house; the gods coveted him. What shall I do? I pray you speak to me. What shall the Okusama do?"

With the aid of Omi, the geisha slowly arose, and, walking blindly toward the screens, opened them at last.

At her sudden appearance the maidens supporting and restraining the Okusama drew back, and even the wild wife of Matsuda stopped her bitter crying for a moment, for a faint smile was on the lips of the Spider, and she held out both her hands toward them.

"Silence is good," she gently admonished. "It is necessary to think. Help me all, I pray you!"

They followed her into the chamber and seated themselves in a solemn little circle about her. Presently:

"Last night the honorable Lord Taro slept safe upon your bosom, Okusama?"

The poor wife of the geisha-keeper clasped her thin hands passionately upon her breast; but her expression was less wild, her words intelligible.

"Here, my Moonlight! In my arms, the soft head nestling beneath my chin—so warm—so—so—so-o—"

She laid her hands in the place where the little head had rested. Her features worked as if she must again abandon herself to anguished weeping, but the look on Moonlight's face restrained her with almost hypnotic power.

"It was after the going of the master?" she queried, speaking very slowly and gently, as if thus the better to secure intelligent answers.

"After the going," repeated the woman. "For good-fortune I held him in the andon-light, that his honorable face might be the last my lord should see as he departed."

"He has gone to the—city?"

"To the city. He contemplated arousing the interest of a departing regiment in your honorable presence here, but, alas!" She broke down again, crying out piercingly that the evil ones had come meanwhile in the absence of the master of the house, and who was there left save helpless females to seek the august little one?

Moonlight's chin had fallen into her hands again. She seemed to think deeply, but the stricken, numb look was gone. Two red spots crept into her cheeks, and her dark eyes gleamed dangerously.

She was rehearsing in her mind the words and actions of Matsuda since his return. She was acutely aware of the base character of the geisha-keeper, and recalled the many times when she had seen him plunged in calculating thought, pacing and repacing the gardens, gnawing like a rat at his nails, and ever his eye stealing craftily to her.

Suddenly there came clearly to the geisha what had possessed for days the mind of the master. Like an illuminating flash from the gods it came upon her what Matsuda had done with her child.

There arose now before her agonized vision the cruel, scornful face of the fearful mother-in-law, and beside it the round, envious, malicious countenance of Ohano. Like a meek, mute fool, she had permitted them to drive her from her rightful—yes, her legal—home, because she had not then known her full power. Now they had stolen from her the one link that bound her inexorably to the beloved dead: for Japanese women believe their soldiers dead until they return. Little they knew of the true character of the Spider! She would show them that even one of the vagabond, despised actor race from which she had come was not to be trodden upon with impunity.

She sprang to her feet, electrified with her new purpose. The geishas scattered, alarmed and frightened, on either side of her.

"Okusama!" She caught at the woman's wandering attention as the latter raised herself from her prostrate position on the floor.

"My Moonlight?"

"You have jewels—cash, perhaps! Speak!"

The troubled brows of the Okusama drew together, and the vague look of wandering came back to her eyes. Moonlight dropped on her knees opposite the woman, and, placing her hands on her shoulders, forced her to look directly in her face.

"Answer me—speak, Okusama!"

As still the poor creature regarded her vaguely, the geisha whispered with entreating tenderness:

"Tell me—my—mother!"

Over the wild features of the Okusama a gentle, wistful smile crept.

"What shall I say?" she plaintively whispered.

"Name your possessions. He has given you jewels, money even. Yes, it is so—is it not?"

The woman nodded. Her lips began to quiver like a child about to cry. The geishas and the apprentices had crowded in a circle about them, and now they seemed to hang in suspense upon the words of the Okusama.

"It is—so!" she faintly said.

"Will you not give them to me?" pleaded the Spider. Then, as the woman drew back timorously, she cried: "Quick, now, while you remember where they are!"

Her eyes were on the Okusama's, hypnotically compelling her. Slowly the woman tottered to her feet. She staggered across the room, supported on either side by the geishas. She came to the east wall, felt along it till her fingers found a secret panel, pushed it aside, found an inner one, and still an inner one, and still an inner one. Then she drew out the lacquer safe, and, with a conciliating smile trembling over her vacant features, she opened the casket and poured the jewels into the lap of the Spider. Moonlight looked at them with glittering eyes of excitement. Then she spoke to the geishas.

"You all have heard of Oka, the great and just judge of feudal days. You know how it was he decided the parentage of a child whom two women claimed. He bade them each take an arm of the girl and pull, and the strongest should prevail to keep the child. Alas, the poor mother dared not pull too hard lest she hurt her beloved offspring, and preferred to resign her child to the impostor. Thus the judge knew she was the true mother. Maidens, in the city of Kioto there are judges as wise as Oka, but much money is needed to obtain the services of those who must bring the cases before them. Come, little Omi, we set out now upon a long and perilous journey!"

"The gods go with you!" quavered the geishas, wiping their tears upon their sleeves.

"Ah, may all the gods lead and protect you!" sobbed the Okusama.

XXII

They were bathing the young Lord Saito Taro: the Lady Saito Ichigo and a rosy-cheeked country girl who had recently entered the family's service. Indeed, the coming of the child had materially altered the regimen of the household. The servants that had been cast aside, as a pious sign from the women that they desired to share their lord's sacrifices during war-time, were now restored, or their places were filled by new maids.

There was an air of activity throughout the entire estate; the maids bustled about swiftly, the chore-boy whistled at his toil, and the aged gateman looked up from the great Western book into which he seemed to bury his nose at all times.

The little Taro lay upon his grandmother's lap, and she rubbed his shining little body with warm towels, tendered by the admiring maids.

There was a curious change in the face of Lady Saito. Almost it seemed as if an iron had been pressed across her features, smoothing away the harsh and bitter lines. The eyes had lost their angry luster, and seemed almost mild and peaceful in expression as she raised them for a moment to give an order to the nursemaid. She chuckled contentedly when the baby grasped at her thumb and put it into his diminutive mouth, sucking upon it with fervor and relish.

Every slight movement of its face or body delighted and moved her to an emotion new and fascinating. Indeed, she was experiencing in the little Taro all the maternal emotions she had sternly denied herself with her own son.

From the moment when she had taken the warm tiny body into her arms everything within her seemed to have capitulated; this in spite of the fact that she did not wish to love, had not intended to love, this child of the Spider!

Now the Spider, and all the bitter animosity and shame she had brought into the proud family of the Saitos, were forgotten. This was the child of her son, the Lord Saito Gonji! Its eyes were the eyes of her son—its mouth, its chin, even its gentle expression; she traced hungrily every seeming likeness, and proclaimed the fact that her son had indeed been reborn to her in the little Taro.

The youngest of the nursemaids was a bright-eyed, somewhat forward girl who had obtained employment recently by cajoling the honorable cook, now factotum of the household. In the eyes of Ochika, wife of the cook, the girl was an impudent minx, who should have been sent flying from a respectable household. Ochika even penetrated from her domain of the kitchen, to the presence of the Lady Saito Ichigo, in order to whisper into the lady's somewhat absent ear a tale of unseemly dances and songs indulged in by the nursemaid for the delectation of the other servants.

Omi (the nurse-girl's name) seemed, however, so innocent and childish in appearance that the Lady Saito was loath to believe her guilty of anything more than a naughty desire to tease Ochika, whose jealousy of her good-looking husband was so notorious among the servants that it was a never-failing source of both merriment and strife. What, however, in Omi recommended her chiefly to the fond grandmother was the fact that the honorable Lord Taro appeared to love her, and was never so happy as when upon his nurse's back.

Now, as Omi danced her hand playfully across his round and shining little stomach, Taro roared with delight, and tossed up his tiny pink heels in approbation. So noisy, so continued, so absolutely joyous was his crowing laughter that the face of his grandmother melted into a smile.

The smile, however, wavered uneasily and was soon suppressed as Ohano silently entered the room. The girl's face was ashen in color, her eyes more like mere slits than ever. She stood leaning against the shoji, her expression sullen and lowering, her attitude similar to that of a spoiled and angry child.

"Ohayo gozarimazu!" murmured the mother-in-law, politely; and she was angrily aware of the conciliating tone in her voice, she who was accustomed to command.

"Ohayo!" The girl flung back the morning greeting, almost as if it were a challenge.

"Well," said her mother, sharply. "Be good enough to take the place of Omi. It will do your heart good to rub the honorable body of your"— she paused and met the scowling glance of Ohano—"your lord's child," she finished.

Omi was tendering the towels; but Ohano ignored the pert little maid. She crossed the room deliberately and slowly sank upon her knees opposite Lady Saito and the baby. Omi was watching the scene with absorbed interest, and she jumped at the sharp voice of Lady Saito.

"To your other duties, maiden!" admonished her mistress, conscious of the fact that the girl was watching Ohano intently.

Alone with the child and Ohano, she began in a complaining voice:

"Now it is most uncivilized to permit one's emotions to show upon the honorable face, which should be a mask as regards all inner feelings. I advise stern control of all angry impulses. Cultivate graciousness of heart, and do not forget each day properly to thank the gods for putting into your arms the honorable child of your lord."

Said Ohano in a breathless whisper, while her bosom heaved up and down tempestuously:

"He is the child of the—Spider! Take care lest he sting thy breast too, mother-in-law!"

The older woman drew the warm towels about the baby, almost as if for protection.

"He is my son's child," she said, hoarsely. "Envy and malice are traits we women are warned repeatedly against in the 'Greater Learning for Women.'"

"He is the Spider's child!" almost chanted Ohano, and she put her lame hand to her throat as though it pained her. "His eyes are identical with hers!"

"Nay," said her mother-in-law, gently; "then you have not looked into the eyes of the little one. I pray you do so, Ohano. It will soften your heart, for, see, they are duplicates of the eyes of your lord!"

She turned the child's head about so that its smiling, friendly glance met Ohano's.

For a moment the latter stared at him, her lips working, her eyes widened. The baby had paused in his laughter and was studying the working features of his stepmother with infantile gravity. Almost unconsciously, as if fascinated, she bent lower above him, and as she did so he reached up a little hand and grasped at her face. A smile broke over his rosy features, displaying the two little teeth within and showing every adorable dimple encrusted in its fair features.

The breath came from Ohano in gasps. All of a sudden she threw up her arm blindly, almost a motion of defense. Then with a wordless sob she put her face upon the floor. She wept stormily, as one whose whole forces are bent upon finding an outlet. For a time there was no sound in the chamber save that of the moaning Ohano.

The child had fallen asleep, and Lady Saito kept her eyes fixed upon his round, charming little face. She would let Ohano's passion spend itself. These daily outbursts since the coming of the child were becoming intolerable, she thought. She had been too lenient with

Ohano. It would be necessary soon to teach the girl her exact position in the household.

As she looked at the beautiful, sleeping child the sudden thought of parting with it seized horribly upon her. Her face twitched like some hideous piece of parchment suddenly animated with life. Nothing, she told herself fiercely—neither the clamoring voice of the wild mother, nor the sulky jealousy of Ohano—should cause her now to relinquish her hold upon the descendant of the illustrious ancestors. Let the Spider do her worst! Let the vindictive jealousy of Ohano betray to the world the truth! She, the Lady Saito Ichigo, would defy them all. The gates of Saito should be sealed and guarded as rigorously as if these were feudal days. As for Ohano! She looked at the girl with a new expression. Between her and the little one resting upon her bosom there could be but one choice.

"My girl," she said to Ohano, finally, "dry your face, if you please. It is unseemly for one of gentle birth to abandon one's self to passion. Come, come, there is a limit to my patience!"

Ohano sat up sullenly, drying her eyes with the ends of her sleeve. The Lady Saito was choosing her words carefully, and her stern glance never wavered as she bent it upon Ohano's quivering face.

"Without my lord's child, Ohano, you are but a cipher in the house of the ancestors. It would become necessary to serve you as once we served an innocent one before you!"

Ohano's hand clutched at her bosom. She appeared to be suffocating, and could hardly speak the words:

"You do not mean—you dare not mean—that you would divorce me!"

"The law is clear in your case, as in that of your predecessor," said her mother, coldly.

"I will speak to my uncle Takedo Isami. I will address all of my honorable relatives. I will tell them with what you have threatened me, the daughter of samourai! You have compared me with a geisha—a Spider! It is intolerable—not to be borne!"

"Nay," vigorously defended her mother-in-law. "You speak not now of a geisha, Ohano, but—of—the mother of the last descendant of the illustrious ancestors."

A silence fell between them, broken only by the breathing of Ohano—short, gasping, indrawn sobs which she seemed no longer able to control.

Presently, when she was quieter, her mother-in-law put a question roughly to the girl.

"What is it to be, Ohano? Will you accept the child of the Lord Saito Gonji, proclaiming it to be your own, defying the very world to take it from you, or—?"

Ohano's face was turned away. Her head was swimming, and she felt strangely weak. After a moment she said in a very faint voice, as if the last trace of resistance within her had been victoriously beaten out by her mother-in-law:

"I serve the ancestors of the Saito—and my Lord Saito Gonji!"

XXIII

Ohano did not leave her room all of the following day. A maid brought word to Lady Saito that her daughter-in-law wished to meditate and pray alone. Permission was somewhat ungraciously granted. Her "moods," as Lady Saito termed them, had become a source of irritation. However, the proposition to "meditate and pray" was good. Ohano, perchance, would profit by her thoughts and emerge a reasonable being.

At noon the soft-hearted little Omi begged to be permitted to take tea and refreshments to Ohano. She was gone some time, to the aggravation of her mistress, for the little Taro was loudly demanding his favorite's return. When at last, however, the girl returned, she brought such a message to her mistress that the latter forgot everything else in the glow of satisfaction. Ohano asked for the Lord Saito Taro.

Little Omi hurried out with the child in her arms. She paused upon the threshold for a moment and threw a curious glance back at her mistress. Lady Saito's face was wreathed in smiles, even while the tears dropped like rain down her withered cheeks. The girl hid her excited face against the child's little body, then, almost running, she sped from the room.

It was very lonely for Lady Saito the rest of that day. She did not wish to disturb Ohano, but how hungrily her heart longed for the return of her baby! How she missed it, even during the short period it had been gone.

In the middle of the afternoon, when she had fallen into a drowsy reverie upon her mat, she was disturbed by the sudden shoving aside of a screen behind her. She turned her head and saw in the aperture the agitated face of Kiyo, the gateman. He had fallen to his knees, and now crawled on them toward her. Something in his abject attitude awoke within the breast of his mistress a sickening fear of a calamity he had come to report. She felt as if paralyzed, unable either to stir or to utter a word.

Undoubtedly the gateman brought bad tidings, for his place was not in the house, and it was an unheard-of thing for one in his position to force his way into the august presence of the mistress. She said to herself:

"He has come to report the death of my dear son or of my husband!"

Vainly she put back her hand for the support of Ohano, but the girl was still secluded in her chamber.

"Speak!" she gasped, at last. "I command you not to hesitate!"

Despite the peremptory words, she was shaking like one in an illness. Her knees gave way. She sank down upon them in a collapsed heap. She looked entreatingly at the retainer, who seemed unable or unwilling to answer her.

"You bring exalted and joyous news from Tenshi-sama!" she cried, brokenly. "I pray you speak the words!"

"Nay, mistress!" His tremulous old voice shook, and he could not control the shaking of his aged limbs. He had been in the service of the Lady Saito since her babyhood. "It is of the youngest Lord Saito I speak!"

"My son! Gonji!"

"Thy honorable grandson, mistress," he corrected.

She stared at him, aghast.

"Baby-san!" She was upon her feet now, with the strength and savagery of a mother at bay. "He is here in the shiro!"

The gateman looked at her mutely.

"He has been stolen—by the maiden Omi. It is said she was in the service of the first Lady Saito Gonji."

For a moment Lady Saito stared at the man with unbelieving eyes. Suddenly she clapped her hands loudly, but no smiling-faced, sharp-tongued Omi came running fleetly to her service. Only the swollen-eyed wife of the cook crept into the room.

"*Thou* knowest where—" She could not continue. Her words choked her.

"Nay, I do not know," burst out Ochika. "She was an imp of the lowest Hades. Maledictions upon her! May Futen tear her flesh!"

"Hush!" cried Lady Saito, with a sudden violence; and almost aloud she shouted the words:

"It is the rod of the gods! From the decree of Heaven there is no escape!"

She became conscious that Ohano was beside her. She looked at the girl strangely, and as she did so something in Ohano's eyes revealed the truth to her. She shrank from her daughter-in-law with a motion almost of loathing.

"Why, Ohano!" she cried. "It was *thou* who sent for—it is—"

Ohano turned from her abruptly and moved briskly toward the gateman.

"It was thy duty," she haughtily censured, "to pursue and seize the woman."

"Her feet had wings, august young mistress. With the honorable young lord upon her back she fairly flew by the gates, as if possessed of infernal power."

"And thou art very old!" said the Lady Saito, gently. "Thy ancient limbs are unable to compete with the fleet wings of a mother's love!"

XXIV

At the evening meal, which was served upon an open balcony because of the intense heat, Ohano kept her eyes assiduously upon her food. The mood of her mother-in-law had changed. There was nothing gentle in her expression now as she savagely stabbed at the live fish upon her plate, speared it in just the proper place, and then lifted a morsel of the still palpitating flesh upon her chop-stick.

"This is excellent fish, Ohano," she said, pleasantly. "Come, taste a morsel while the live flavor is still upon it. Possibly it will remind you of the brevity of life. Now we are here, possessed of tempestuous passions and emotions—for even a fish, so it is said, has the soul of a murderer. Then just think, one sharp pick of the knife—or sword—and, like the honorable fish, we are—gone! The devils of hatred, envy, desire, and malice can no longer torture us!"

Ohano said nothing. She gave one swift glance at the fish, then turned away, nauseated.

Lady Saito grunted and fell to eating her meal as if hungry. Presently, filled and refreshed, she began again:

"Of course it must be very plain to you, Ohano, that it will be impossible for the Saitos to regain possession of my son's child unless we take into our household the mother also."

Ohano sat up with a start, and as her mother-in-law continued, the expression of intense fear on her face deepened.

"I know of no law in Japan—and I have been advised in the matter—by which we can forcibly take a child from its mother, in the absence of its father."

Ohano did not move. She moistened her dry lips, and her eyes moved furtively. She watched her mother-in-law's face with a mute expression, half of terror and half of defiance. In the going of the hated child of the Spider, Ohano had not found the relief she had expected. Nay, there loomed before her now the possibility of a greater menace to her peace of mind. She felt the weight of the older woman's tyrannical will as never before. She stammered:

"Pardon my dullness. I do not understand your words."

"It is better," counseled the other, sternly, "that you not alone understand my words, but that you study them well! Think awhile, Ohano!"

For a time there was silence between them; then Lady Saito continued:

"It is my wish, it is the wish of the ancestors, that the honorable descendant of the Saitos be housed here in the home of his fathers. If it is impossible to have my son's son without the legal custodian of his body, then we must face the matter gracefully, and solicit her, humbly if need be, to come also!"

"That—would be—impossible!" gasped Ohano.

"Nay," protested her mother, coldly, "it is done every day in Japan. The honorable Moonlight will not be the first divorced wife who has been again received in the home of the parents-in-law. You forget that until recently there was even a custom among many families where the wife failed in her duty to supply children to her husband, for an honorable concubine to be chosen in her place duly to serve her lord."

Ohano tried to smile, but it was a ghastly effort.

"That is an ancient custom. It is no longer tolerated in Japan. It would be a matter of notorious gossip. We could not, with honor, she and I, live under the same roof together."

"That is true," admitted Lady Saito, calmly, and now she met Ohano's eyes firmly.

"I refuse to be 'returned,'" cried Ohano, shrilly. "My honorable relatives will not permit you to divorce me for such a cause. It is not possible to treat me in the manner accorded a geisha!"

"That, too, is true," quietly assented her mother-in-law. "We, the Saitos, desire to remain on terms of friendship with your most honorable family. Now, therefore, we look to you, Ohano, for a solution of the problem. You are right. These are not the times when honorable men maintain concubines under the same roofs as their wives. We wish to impress the Western people with our morality! Ha!" she broke off, to laugh bitterly. "We follow the code set by them. Yet what are we to do when confronted by such a condition as exists in our household now? When a wife is childless, it is surely an excellent rule which allows a humble one to bear the offspring and put them into the arms of the exalted but childless wife. But we can do this no longer. Our war with Russia—our victories, which are proclaimed daily—will make these matters all the more a sensitive point with the nation. We must live according to the code set down by the Westerners, as I have said. They have taught us to fight! Our people desire to imitate their virtues!" She laughed in hoarse derision. Then she continued:

"We bow, then, to this. It cannot be helped. Now, as we cannot take the honorable Lord Taro by force from his mother, and we cannot permit two wives of my son to remain under the one roof, we must seek some other solution of our problem. Can you not offer some suggestion?"

"It is possible," said Ohano, "that the Lord Saito Gonji may not give up his life for Tenshi-sama. Many soldiers return. In that event—" She stammered piteously. "I am young and very healthy. I will bear him children yet!"

"We cannot count upon so unlikely a contingency, my girl. We Japanese women, when we sacrifice our men to the Emperor's service, *pray* that they may not return! It is a pious, patriotic prayer, Ohano. Be worthy of it, my girl. Duty and honor to the ancestors are the watchwords of our language."

"Duty—and honor!" repeated Ohano, slowly.

A long silence fell between them, during which Ohano's eyes never left the face of her mother-in-law. A sick terror assailed her, so that she could not move, but sat there rigidly, nursing her lame arm. What dreadful project, she asked herself, did the stern mother-in-law now meditate, that she should look at the unhappy Ohano with such a peculiar, commanding expression?

Finally the older woman said, with quiet force:

"Ohano, you come of illustrious stock. There have been women of your race who have found a solution to problems more tragic than yours. I pray you reflect upon the text of the samourai, which, as you know, was as binding upon the women as the men: 'To die with honor, when one can no longer live with honor!'"

She stood up, and leaned heavily upon her staff.

"Let me recommend," she added, softly, "that you study and emulate— and *emulate*"—she repeated the last word with deadly emphasis—"the lives of your ancestors!"

Ohano's mouth had dropped wide open. She came to her feet mechanically, and mechanically she backed from her mother-in-law until she came to the farthest screen; and against this she leaned like one about to faint.

Her mother-in-law's voice seemed to reach her as from very far away, and also it seemed to Ohano that a smile, jeering and cruel, was on the aged woman's face, marking it like a livid scar. It was as if she cried to Ohano:

"I challenge you, as the daughter of a samourai, to do your duty!"

Ohano gasped out something, she knew not what.

"Ho!" cried Lady Saito, fiercely, "it does not matter to the true daughter of a samourai whether the days of suppuku are passed or not. We take refuge too much behind the new rules of life. The spark of heroes is imperishable. If you are a worthy daughter of your ancestors it is still within your insignificant body!"

Said Ohano, with chattering teeth:

"I—I—will—go—to the go-down (treasure-house), honorable mother-in-law, and study the swords of my ancestors. I pray you ask the gods to give me strength!"

When she was gone, the Lady Saito Ichigo summoned a maid. To her she said curtly:

"You will bid the Samourai Asado"—it was the first time in years she had referred to this old retainer as "samourai"—"unlock the doors of the honorable go-down. The Lady Saito Gonji would examine the treasure-chests of her ancestors!"

XXV

In the go-down itself, Ohano's courage deserted her completely. As the stone doors of the go-down were pushed aside, and she stepped into the darkened chamber with its odor almost as of dead things, a sense of unconquerable repugnance and terror assailed her.

From every side, gleaming, softly smiling almost, in the light of the setting sun, the ancient relics of bygone days were heaped. Almost it seemed as if these beautiful objects were living things, their burnished and lacquered bodies afire in the darkened chamber.

Slowly, fearfully, staggering as she walked, Ohano made her way between rows of this piled-up treasure, the wealth and pride of the house of Saito.

Now she had come to where the possessions of her own honorable family were set. Trembling in every limb, hovering and hesitating above it, she at length unlocked and opened an ancient chest. Fearfully she looked down into its depths, then felt below the heavy layers of silk. Presently, with her poor, lame hand, Ohano brought up a single sword.

It was very long. The hilt was of lacquer, a shining black. The ferrule, guard, cleats, and rivets were inlaid and embossed with rare metals. The beautiful blade, as brittle as an icicle, seemed to shine in the darkened chamber with its noble classic beauty, and it awoke in the breast of the agitated Ohano a new sensation—one of awe, of reverence and pride!

She held it in the light that came through the still open door, and for long she looked at it with widened, fascinated eyes.

It seemed to her that some chanted song of proud and noble achievements rang in her ears, as if the whispering ghosts of her ancestors were urging her on.

"Courage!" they cried to her. "The gods love thee now!"

She pricked her wrist to test her strength. Then she screamed harshly, like one who has lost his senses. The sword dropped with a clank upon the stone floor. Ohano fled from the go-down like one possessed.

With the blood streaming from her hands and marking her progress with its ruddy drops, she sped across the gardens and into the house. No one stopped her; no one even called to her. All had been sent away by orders of the Lady Saito Ichigo.

Alone again in her chamber, with her breath coming in agitated gasps, her wrist burning with an unbearable pain, weak from the loss of blood, she swayed by the shoji, her dry lips reiterating the common prayer of the devout Buddhist: "Namu, amida, Butsu!" (Save us, eternal Buddha!)

Suddenly she felt something cool placed within her hands, and her fingers were pressed gently but forcibly about the object. It was the sword she had left behind. A superstitious fear assailed her that the gods had perceived her weakness and inexorably had placed the sword within her hands, demanding of Ohano that she do her duty.

Within the girl's breast a new emotion arose—the ambition to prove to all the ancestors that within her weak and insignificant body yet glowed the spark of heroism; that she was, after all, a true daughter of the samourai.

Her hands acquired a miraculous steadiness and strength. She set the sword firmly before her, point up. Grasping it with both hands about the middle, she dumbly, and with a certain dignity and even grace, rested her body upon it. Slowly she sank down the full length of the blade.

XXVI

Meanwhile, within the war-torn heart of Manchuria, the last words of Ohano came up to torment the soldier. His days and nights were made horrible by the imagined reiteration in his ears of the words of Ohano.

By the light of a hundred camp-fires he saw the face of Moonlight, the wife he had discarded at the command of the ancestors. He tried to picture it as he had first seen her, with that peculiar radiance about her beauty. She had appeared to him then like to some rare and precious flower, so fragile and exquisite it seemed almost profanation to touch her. How he had desired her! How he had adored her!

He recalled, with anguish, the first days of their marriage—a mixture of exquisite joy and pain; then the harrowing, heartbreaking months that had followed—the metamorphosis that had taken place in his beautiful wife. How timid, meek, submissive, they had made her in those latter days! He paced and repaced the ground, suffering torments incomparably worse than those of the wounded soldiers.

To think of Moonlight as an inmate of the Yoshiwara, as Ohano had insisted, the last resource of the most abandoned of lost souls, was to arouse him to an inner frenzy that no amount of action in the bloodiest encounters could even temporarily efface.

He began to count the days which must pass before his release. He knew by now that the war was soon to end. Already negotiations were under way. At first he had bitterly regretted the fact that the gods had not mercifully permitted him to give up his life; now he realized that perchance they had saved it for another purpose—the purpose of finding his lost wife. He would devote the rest of his life, he promised himself, to this undertaking; and, ah! when once again they two should meet, nothing should part them.

They would go away to a new land—a better land even than Japan—of which he had heard so much from a friend he had made out here in Manchuria. There men did not cast off their wives because they were childless. There no cruel laws sacrificed an innocent wife at the demand of the dead. There there were no licensed dens of inquity into which the innocent might be sold into a bondage lower than hell itself!

Gonji dreamed unceasingly of this land of promise, whither he intended to go when once he had found his beloved Moonlight.

Incognito, finally, the Lord Gonji returned to Japan. He did not, as became a dutiful and honorable son, proceed straightway to his home, there to permit the members of his family to celebrate and rejoice over his return.

At last Lord Gonji felt free of the thrall of the ancestors. He was a son of the New Japan, master of his own conscience and deeds. The old strict code set down for men of his class and race he knew was medieval, childish, unworthy of consideration. Hitherto his actions had been governed by the example of the ancestors and by order of those in authority over him. Now he was free—free to choose his own path; and his path led not to the house of his fathers.

It led, instead, to that "hell city" which had been imprinted so vividly upon his mind that even in the heart of Manchuria he had seen its lights and heard its brazen music.

From street to street of the Yoshiwara, and from house to house, now went the Lord Saito Gonji, scanning with eager, feverish eyes every pitiful little inmate thus publicly exhibited in cages. But among the hopeless, apathetic faces that smiled at him with enforced beguilement was not the one he sought.

He turned to other cities, wherever the famous brothels were maintained, leaving for the last his home city of Kioto, where once the Spider had been the darling of the House of Slender Pines.

How his haughty relatives had despised her calling; yet how desirable, how infinitely superior it was in every way to the one to which they had perhaps driven her.

The geisha was protected under the law, and her virtue was in her own hands. She could be as pure or as light as she chose. Not even the harshest of masters could actually drive her to the degradation of the inmates of the Yoshiwara, who were sold into bondage often in their babyhood.

If he could but believe that Moonlight was now in the House of Slender Pines! Yet his agents had insisted she had not returned to her former home: moreover, they had supported the contention of Ohano, that undoubtedly it was into some such resort that the unhappy outcast had finally been driven.

Upon a day when the inmates of the Yoshiwara of Kioto were upon their annual parade, when the city was swept by a paroxysm of patriotic enthusiasm over the return of the victorious troops, Saito Gonji, worn and wearied from his vain quest through many cities, returned at last to his home city.

The streets were in holiday dress. From every roof-tree and tower the sun-flag tossed its ruddy symbol in the air. The people ran through the streets as if possessed, now cheering the passing soldiers, now waving and shouting to the happy paraders, and all following, some taunting, some cheering the long line of courtezans of the Yoshiwara.

They marched in single file, their long, silken robes, heavily embroidered, held up by their maids, and accompanied by their diminutive, toddling apprentices, often little girls as young as six and seven.

Yet, small as they were, each was a miniature reproduction and understudy of her mistress, in her elaborate coiffure with its glittering ornaments (the geisha wears flowers), her obi tied in front, and the thick paste of paint laid lividly from brow to chin. Some day it would be their lot to step into the place of the ones they emulated, and, in turn, slaves would hold their trains and masters would exhibit them like animals in public cages.

Gonji followed the long train of courtezans for miles. Sometimes he would run ahead, and, walking backward, pass down the long line, scanning every face piercingly and letting not one escape his scrutiny. And, as he studied the faces of these "hell women," as his countrymen had named them, for the first time Gonji forgot his beloved Moonlight. The words of the American officer he had met in the campaign in Manchuria came up vividly to his mind:

"No nation," the American had said, "can honorably hold its head erect among civilized nations, no matter what its prowess and power, so long as its women are held in such bondage; so long as its women are bartered and sold, often by their own fathers, husbands, and brothers, like cattle."

A great and illuminating light broke upon the tempest-tossed soul of the Lord Saito Gonji. He would erect an imperishable monument to the memory of his lost wife. She should be the inspiration for the most knightly act that had ever been performed in the history of his nation.

It should be his task to effect the abolishment of the Yoshiwara! He would devote his life to this one great cause, and never would he abandon it until he had succeeded. This, and the revision of the inhuman and barbarous laws governing divorce, should be his life-work.

He would show the ancestors that there were deeds even more worthy and heroic than those of the sword.

XXVII

If Ohano's relatives were aware of the manner of her death, they gave no sign. Such of the male members of the family and of her husband's as were not serving in the war stolidly attended the funeral of their kinswoman, and shortly Ohano was honorably interred in the mortuary halls of the Saito ancestors.

There had been expressions of sorrow over her passing, but these were largely perfunctory. Ohano had been an orphan; and, as she had lived all of her life in the Saito house, her husband's people had really been nearer to her than her own family. Her uncle, Takedo Isami, was possibly the only one of her relatives who had known the girl with any degree of intimacy, and at this time he too had entered the war service.

Many offerings and prayers were put up for Ohano, and in the end the relatives quietly dispersed to their homes, leaving the silent and prim old Lady Saito alone in the now almost deserted mansion. She shut herself into the chamber of the dead girl, and for several days not even her personal maid was permitted to intrude upon her voluntary retirement. Whatever were the thoughts that tormented and haunted the mother-in-law of Ohano, she emerged, in the end, still resolute and stern, though her hair had turned as white as snow.

From day to day now the aged lady crouched over the kotatsu, warming her withered old fingers, lighting and relighting her pipe, and always seeming to listen, to watch for some one she expected to return.

Couriers and agents had been despatched by her orders to the city in search of Moonlight and her child. There was nothing left for the Dowager Saito to do, save to wait. Not for a moment had she considered the possibility that her servants might be unable to find the one they sought, or, having found her, fail to induce the geisha to return to the house of the Saitos. To keep her mind from brooding over Ohano, she endeavored to force it to remain fixed upon one matter only—the recovery of her son's child.

But the days passed away, the chill season of hoar frost swept the trees bare of leaf and color, and the silently moving servants set the winter amado (wooden sliding walls) in place; and still, with a stony, frozen look upon her face, the Lady Saito waited.

Gradually the proud and strong spirit within her began to weaken under the strain. Supported by a maid on either side, she toiled up the mountain slope to visit the temple endowed by her family, and to seek advice and comfort there. In broken words, her voice stammering and shaking, she whispered a confession to the chief priest, and entreated him to help her with spiritual advice and prayers.

Though the lives of the priests are devoted largely to meditation and the study of the sacred books, they are by no means ignorant of what passes about them. The chief priest of the Saito temple knew every detail of the casting out of the first wife; he knew, moreover, what had been the end of Ohano. As the family had not, up to the present, however, sought his advice in the matter, he had expressed no opinion.

An acolyte had quite recently come to the chief priest with a strange story. It concerned a very beautiful geisha who seemed in deep distress, who, with her maiden clinging to her skirt and a baby upon her back, had asked the boy to direct them toward a certain small temple where an ancient priestess of the Nichi sect had lived. The acolyte had been unable to direct the geisha; and, to his surprise and distress, the two had climbed higher up the mountain slope, with the evident intention of penetrating farther into the interior. Both the priest and the acolyte had waited anxiously for the return of the wanderers, for they knew there were no sheltering places in the direction the pair had taken, and the weather had turned very cold. It was not the season for an infant to be abroad. Now the chief priest called the acolyte before him and requested the boy to repeat his story to the Lady Saito Ichigo.

She listened with mixed feelings; and when the boy was through he chanced, timidly, to raise his eyes to the face of the exalted patroness of the temple, and, as he afterward informed the priest, he saw that great tears ran down the stern and furrowed cheeks of the lady, nor could she speak for the sobs that tore her.

XXVIII

The trees had dropped their leaves, and, with naked arms extended, seemed to speak voicelessly of the winter almost come. Only the evergreen pines kept their warm coats of green, and under their shade the travelers found a temporary refuge from the wind and the cold, piercing rain.

Moonlight had been very sure that they had climbed the hill in which was hidden the retreat of the nun who had previously harbored her, and where she knew she could find a refuge to which not even the agents of the Saito might penetrate. But Kioto is surrounded by hills on all sides, and the geisha had lost her way.

With the little Omi to run before her and sell to the chance passer-by or pilgrim, for a sen or two, the jewels of the crazed wife of Matsuda, or to beg rice and fish from charitably disposed temples, they had subsisted thus far.

At first she had turned a deaf ear to the entreaties of her maiden, that they go to the city below rather than to the bleak, deserted, autumn hills. But now, as the penetrating rain searched down through even the wide-spreading branches of the pine-trees, her heart ached heavily.

Omi, shivering against her mistress's side, began to cry, and recommenced her prayers to return to the city below. The troops were returning, and even here on the quiet hillside the sound of the beating drum, the wild and hoarse singing, and cheering of the soldiers and the citizens was heard.

"Why perish in the cold hills?" asked the little apprentice-geisha, "when the warm, happy city calls to us? Oh, let us go! Let us go!"

Feeling the cold hands of her baby, the geisha shivered; yet as she looked off hungrily to where the little maiden pointed she felt a sense of strong reluctance almost akin to terror. It was down there they were looking for her, she knew. There they would take from her the honorable child of her beloved lord.

"How much colder it is getting," reproached Omi, crossly; "and see, graciousness, your kimono is not even padded."

"Undo my obi, Omi. Wrap it about yourself and his lordship. It is seven yards long, and will protect you both amply."

"But you, sweet mistress? I will not take your obi. Your hands are cold. The august clogs are broken even!"

She knelt to tie the thong firmer, and while still kneeling Omi continued her beseeching.

"Now, if we start downward, we shall travel much quicker. I will bear his lordship on my back. We can reach the city in less than a night and a day. I know a little garden just on the outskirts of Kioto. There we can spend the night. With warm rice and sake and—"

"Hush, Omi, it is impossible."

Omi threw back her head and began to wail aloud, just as a child would have done. The burden of her cry was that she was cold, very cold, and she was very sure that they would all perish in the wet and horrible mountains. The geisha tried vainly to quiet her. At last she said:

"Omi, if you love me, be patient for yet another day. If to-morrow we do not find the shrine of the honorable nun, then—then—" her voice broke, and she turned her face away. Omi caught at her hand and clung to her joyously.

"Oh, you have promised!" Then, as she saw the distress of her mistress, she cried out remorsefully that she was prepared to follow her wherever she desired to go—yes, even if it should prove to be the highest point of the mountains, said the little maid. After a moment, as the geisha made no response, Omi, already regretting her generous outburst, sighed heavily and declared it was very hard. She sat back on her heels, upon the damp ground, and looked off plaintively toward the city below. How she longed for the bright lights of the geisha-house, the chatter and the movement, the dance and the song, the warm quilt under which was hidden the glowing kotatsu, close to which, Omi knew, the geishas would creep at night for comfort. As she felt the drizzling rain and wind and saw nothing but the dark trees about her, her little head drooped upon her breast, and she began to sob drearily again.

Suddenly the Spider bent above the child and patted her softly upon the head.

"Play a little tune upon your samisen, my Omi, and I will sing to you a little song I myself have composed to the honorable baby-san."

Instantly Omi's face cleared. Crouched upon her heels, looking up adoringly at her mistress, she picked upon her instrument, and while the cold rain dripped down upon them the Spider sang:

Neneko, neneko, ya!
Sleep, my little one, sleep,

As the bottomless pit of the ocean,
So is my love so deep!

Neneko, neneko, ya!
Sleep, my little one, sleep!
As the unexplored vasts of Nirvana,
So is my love so deep!

As the softly crooning voice of the dancer stole out upon the air a little cortège which had found its way up the intricate mountain-path halted there in the woods. In silence the runners dropped the shafts of the vehicles. Supported by her maids, the Lady Saito alighted, and tottered painfully up the hill-slope. She stood very still when she saw that little group under the tree, and began to tremble in every limb.

The little Omi saw her first, and with a cry of fear threw her arms protectingly about her mistress, thrusting her thin little body before her, as if to shield the beloved one from harm. Now Moonlight saw her, and for a moment she remained unmoving, staring at the old figure standing there unprotected in the drizzling rain, with arms half extended, the withered old face full of an appeal she had not yet found the courage to utter.

As she looked at the once dreaded lady, Moonlight was conscious of a sense of great calmness and strength. No longer was her being flooded with the wild impulses of resentment and hatred toward her mother-in-law. She knew not why it was so, but her heart felt barren of all feeling save one of overwhelming pity.

Her voice was as calm and gentle as though she had always been a lady of high caste, who had never known a turbulent emotion.

"Thou art unprotected from the rain. I pray you take my place, honorable Lady Saito!"

Now she was at the side of the other, leading her, waiting upon her. Under the sheltering arms of the great pine-trees, so near to each other that their shoulders touched, these two, who had once hated each other so deeply, looked at one another with white faces.

Said the Lady Saito Ichigo, with quivering lips:

"I have made a long journey!"

Said Moonlight, calmly:

"You come to seek your son's son?"

"Nay," said the aged woman, and she put out a trembling hand and caught beseechingly at the arm of the geisha. "I have come for thee, too, my daughter!"

A silence, unbroken save by the sobs of the little Omi, fell now between them. Then said the geisha, very gently:

"Speak your—will—all-highest one. I—I will try to—to serve the honorable ancestors of the Saito, even though it be necessary to make the supreme sacrifice."

Her hands fumbled with the strings that bound the child in its bag upon her back. Now she had swung it round in front. The child's little face, rosy in sleep, rolled back upon her arm. She felt the hungry arms of the woman beside her reaching out irresistibly toward the child; and, though she tried to smile, a sob tore from her lips as she lifted her baby and put it solemnly into the arms of its grandmother. Then she turned her back quickly, and Omi sprang up and received her into her arms.

Suddenly she felt the shaking fingers of the aged woman upon her shoulder. She said, with her face still hidden and her voice muffled by sobs:

"I pray you go, hastily, lest my love prove greater than my strength."

"The journey is long," said Lady Saito. "Let us set out at once, my daughter. I go not back without thee."

Slowly Moonlight put the sheltering arms of Omi from her and turned and looked wistfully, almost hungrily, at her mother-in-law.

"It is—unnecessary," she said, gently. "I pray you forgive the dissension I have already caused in your honorable family. Say to Ohano, from me, that though it is not possible for me to give to her the one who has given to me his eternal vows, yet gladly I resign to her my little son."

A curious look was on the face of the mother-in-law. For a long moment she stood staring up blankly at the geisha. Then she said, in a tone of deadly quiet:

"My daughter Ohano has gone upon—a journey!"

"A journey!" repeated the geisha, lowly. Then, as she saw that look upon the other's face: "Ah, you mean not surely the Long Journey to the Meido?" she cried out, piteously. Lady Saito's head dropped upon her breast. Moonlight felt overwhelmed, dazed, awed. Ohano gone! Ohano, the strong, the triumphant one!

"I entreat you to come with me now," said Lady Saito, simply. "It was the wish of Ohano that you—that you should take her place." She paused, and added quietly: "It was she, my daughter, who made a place for you in the house of the ancestors."

They had lifted her into the carriage. Her head fell back, and she began to weep slow, painful tears that crept down her face and dropped upon the hands of her maiden. Said the latter, joyously:

"See how the gods love you, sweet mistress. See how they have avenged you. See how they destroy your enemies and—"

"Do not speak so," cried her mistress entreatingly. "Only the gods themselves are competent to judge us. I do not weep for myself, but for Ohano, who has been ruthlessly thrust out upon the Long Journey. I would that I could take her place; but all that I can do to help her is to go to the shrines daily and beseech the gods to make easy the travels of Ohano."

XXIX

It was the season of greatest cold. The she hills of Kioto were enwrapped in a garment of snow, and with the glistening sun upon them they looked as beautiful as a dream. The pines and hemlocks seemed to spread out their dark-green arms, as if to support the glorified burden.

The gateman of the Saito shiro, squatting upon his heels, with his face buried in the great, absorbing book of the West, chanced to look up over his bone-rimmed glasses, and saw a lone traveler coming on foot along the path which led to the lodge gates. Kiyo hobbled down to the gates just as the visitor reached them. In a high, thin voice the ancient gateman challenged the traveler. Then, as the latter did not respond to his call, but peered up at him curiously and suddenly, the old retainer began to tremble so violently that his shaking hands could hardly unbar the gates.

As the young man entered, Kiyo dropped upon his knees, and bumped his bald head repeatedly upon the frozen ground, emitting strange little cries of excitement and joy over the return of the long-absent one.

Deeply touched, Gonji, who had always loved old Kiyo, bent over the gateman, patting his head, and finally even assisting him to his feet. He inquired solicitously after the health of Kiyo and his kindred, and then asked how his own family now were. Kiyo had answered joyously and willingly all the inquiries of his master touching upon his own kinsfolk, but at the questions regarding the family he served he became suddenly constrained and wretched. His silence apparently but aroused the further curiosity and anxiety of Gonji. He persisted, his voice becoming almost peremptory in tone.

"I condescended to ask you regarding the health of my family. You do not answer me, good Kiyo-sama! Is there sickness, then, within the shiro?"

"Iya, iya! (No, no!)" hastily protested Kiyo. "All is well. It is good health within the shiro, praise be to the gods!"

Still his questioner noted something strange about the manner in which the gateman avoided his glance. He studied old Kiyo curiously, as though from his own sad reveries, in which he had been absorbed to the exclusion of all else, he had been reluctantly aroused at the thought of possible danger to his people. Gonji had hardened his heart, as he thought, against the ones who were responsible for his unhappiness—nay, who had deliberately cast forth a pure and beautiful soul. Nevertheless, he experienced a sense of uneasiness at the thought that all had not been well with them.

"Come," he urged. "Do not hesitate to confide in your master, good Kiyo-sama. Tell me the news, be it good or bad."

"All is well. All is well," almost sobbingly chanted the gateman. "I pray you enter the shiro. There you will see for yourself."

Gonji turned a bit uneasily toward the house, then halted abruptly.

"I read in your face," he said, "a tale of some calamity to my family. Already I know of my father's glorious sacrifice for Tenshi-sama"—bowing as he spoke the Mikado's name—"for I was with my father at the end. So if it is that—but no, there is something else troubling you, Kiyo. I know you too well not to read your face. Is it my mother?"

His voice broke slightly, and for the first time in years he was conscious of a sense of tenderness toward his mother. She had been the main source of all his misery; but she loved him. This Gonji knew, despite all.

Again Kiyo hastened to reassure him, this time eagerly and proudly.

"Iya, master. Thy mother is in excellent health. Happy, moreover, as never before, with the honorable Lord Taro, thy son, embraced within her arms!"

The young man was staring at him now strangely. He seemed unable to speak or move. A look as of almost troubled awakening was in the face of Gonji. It was as if a thought, long thrust aside, had suddenly recurred to him. During all these agonizing months, when he had wandered about from city to city, he had been possessed with but one idea—the finding of his wife. Now, suddenly, the gateman's words came to him as a very revelation. Strange that he had not even thought upon this matter since he had left Japan. He was a father!

"It is—possible!" he gasped. "I have a—"

"Son! Gloriously a son, master!" cried Kiyo, grinning joyously.

The young man continued to stare almost incredulously at the gateman, but in his face was no reflection of the joy visible in that of the faithful retainer. He was overwhelmed with the sense of a new emotion whose very sweetness tore at his heart, and brought unbidden tears to his eyes.

Suddenly, against his will even, there came vividly before his mind's eye a vision of Ohano as he had seen her last, crawling upon her knees toward him and beating her hands futilely together, as she besought him piteously to permit her to attend him through the dark paths that led to the Lotus Land.

How the gods had comforted the unloved wife, was his thought, and with it came a sense of overwhelming grief and bitterness that they had not shown a similar charity toward the beloved Moonlight. He pictured Ohano, cherished, protected, praised, within the honorable house of Saito, with the long-desired heir of all the illustrious ancestors upon her bosom. Then his mind reverted to the wandering outcast, Moonlight, and a lump rose stranglingly in his throat. As he made his way blindly toward the house, all the pride and joy of fatherhood, which had uplifted him as on a flood but a moment since, seemed to drop from him no less suddenly, leaving him as before, hopeless, uncomforted, and utterly forlorn.

Within the shiro, the Lady Saito Ichigo sat drowsily swaying by the hibachi, ceaselessly smoking, and muttering incoherent prayers for the soul of her lord and for Ohano's. She was very feeble, helpless, and childish now. Her body had lost much of its vigor, and the sternness which had once made her so formidable seemed to have entirely left her.

Moonlight's dark eyes rested upon her with an expression of both pity and anxiety. Suddenly she pushed the little Taro along the smoothly matted floor and whispered coaxing words into the child's ear. He crawled along several paces till he came behind his grandmother. By grasping her obi at the back he was enabled to pull himself to his feet. Now his chubby, warm little face nestled up against Lady Saito's neck. The pipe dropped from her mouth and fell unheeded upon the hearth. She turned hungrily toward the child and drew him passionately to her breast.

Outside the screens Gonji had paused, unable either to enter or to retire. He had resolved, at whatever cost, to resume his forlorn wanderings in search of the lost one, ere finally he should take up the abolition of the Yoshiwara—a task which had seemed to be assigned to him by the very gods themselves. But before going he felt it to be his duty to have a last interview with his mother, and with Ohano, the mother of his child!

Nevertheless he paused outside the screens, feeling unable to combat the sense of reluctance and repugnance to joining that little family he knew was within. How long he remained outside the shoji he could not have told. He debated the advisability of withdrawing without their knowledge of his presence. Kiyo would keep the secret. So would Ochika, whose loud outcry at his advent he had quickly silenced. Gonji felt sure his brief visit might bring merely unrest and unhappiness. It would be kinder both to Ohano and to his mother to go. As his resolve became fixed, he was swept with an anguished longing and desire at least to see, but once, the face of the son the gods had graciously given him.

With infinite caution, lest the sound might be heard by those within, he began to scratch with his nail upon the fusuma, till gradually he had made a small aperture, and to this he applied his eye.

He remained motionless at the shoji. He saw, within, the toddling child, as it made its swift way across the room toward its grandmother; he heard the sob of his mother as she took the child into her embrace; then he saw the face of Moonlight lifted alertly and turned toward where her husband's face was pressed against the screen. She alone had heard, and, intuitively, had guessed the truth. She came slowly to her feet, her lips apart, her wide eyes dark and beautiful with emotion and excitement.

Suddenly the man outside the screens became animated with the strength almost of a madman. He tore violently at the sliding wall, crushing it into its groove. Now he was upon the threshold of the room.

His mother screamed, hoarsely, wildly. But his glance went over her head and by the little wondering child, who had crawled toward him. Gonji saw nothing in the world save the face of that one who had rushed to meet him.

It was much later that they told him of Ohano. At first the girl's sacrifice, for his sake and that of the ancestors, brought from him only an exclamation of pity; he seemed unable to appreciate the facts of the matter. There was no room for a shadow upon his happiness now. They were sitting in the sunlight, that came in a golden stream through the latticed shoji, piercing its way even through the amado. They said little to each other, but upon their faces was a radiance as golden as the sunlight.

Suddenly a tiny shape flickered across the outer wall. It seemed but a moving speck at first upon the water-colored paper; but so insistently did it beat against the wall that the family perceived it was an insect of some kind.

Gonji arose and looked at it curiously, where it fluttered against the outside of the paper wall.

"Why, it is a cicada—and at this time of year!" he said.

Lady Saito laid her pipe upon the hibachi and hobbled across to her son's side, and Moonlight and the little Taro pressed against him on the other. They all watched the moving little shape outside with absorbed interest and wonder.

"I dreamed of a cicada last night," said Lady Saito, uneasily. "It kept flying at my ears, whispering that it could not rest. It is a bad sign. Open the shoji, my son. We can catch it with the sleeve."

He pushed the screen partly open, and the cicada crept along the lacquered latticed wall, beating its little wings and sliding up and down.

Lady Saito slapped at it with the end of her long sleeve, but it fled to the top of the wall. She beat at it with a bamboo broom, and presently it fluttered down and fell upon the floor.

They all hung over the curious little creature, and as they examined it an oppressive feeling of sadness crept upon them.

"How strange is this little cicada," murmured Moonlight, troubled. "See, one of its little wings is much smaller than the other."

"It is a bad sign," repeated the mother, gloomily; and she made as if to step upon the little creature, when Moonlight grasped at her arm and drew her back.

"Do not kill it! Do not kill it!" she cried, in sudden excitement. "Oh, do you not see—it is Ohano, poor Ohano! She has returned to us in this way. There is a message she wishes to bring us."

Even as she spoke the cicada ceased its fluttering and lay very still. A silence fell upon the Saito family. They were oppressed with the sense of being in the presence of one dead.

Said the Lord Saito Gonji, in a very gentle voice:

"What can it be my wife wishes? I would gladly resign my happiness if I could but make easier the lot of Ohano."

"She was always anxious about her next birth," whispered his mother. "Perhaps she desires a Buddhist service especially for her spirit!"

Moonlight had tenderly lifted the little body and put it into a small box.

"Come," she said, simply. "We must set out at once for the temple. The good priest will perform the Segati service, and we will bury Ohano's little body in the grounds of the temple. There surely it will rest in peace!"

THE END

ONOTO WATANNA

A Note About the Author

Winnifred Eaton, (1875–1954) better known by her penname, Onoto Watanna was a Canadian author and screenwriter of Chinese-British ancestry. First published at the age of fourteen, Watanna worked a variety of jobs, each utilizing her talent for writing. She worked for newspapers while she wrote her novels, becoming known for her romantic fiction and short stories. Later, Watanna became involved in the world of theater and film. She wrote screenplays in New York, and founded the Little Theatre Movement, which aimed to produced artistic content independent of commercial standards. After her death in 1954, the Reeve Theater in Alberta, Canada was built in her honor.

A Note from the Publisher

Spanning many genres, from non-fiction essays to literature classics to children's books and lyric poetry, Mint Edition books showcase the master works of our time in a modern new package. The text is freshly typeset, is clean and easy to read, and features a new note about the author in each volume. Many books also include exclusive new introductory material. Every book boasts a striking new cover, which makes it as appropriate for collecting as it is for gift giving. Mint Edition books are only printed when a reader orders them, so natural resources are not wasted. We're proud that our books are never manufactured in excess and exist only in the exact quantity they need to be read and enjoyed.

Discover more of your favorite classics with Bookfinity™.

- Track your reading with custom book lists.
- Get great book recommendations for your personalized Reader Type.
- Add reviews for your favorite books.
- AND MUCH MORE!

Visit **bookfinity.com** and take the fun Reader Type quiz to get started.

Enjoy our classic and modern companion pairings!